"Don't move," Rand ordered in a harsh whisper.

"Don't talk. No matter what happens."

"Maybe he can give us a ride back to camp," Serene said.

"He's part of an illegal mining operation. Now, be quiet before he decides to shoot first and ask questions later."

Brie began to whimper. Through the veil of branches, Kate watched as the ATV stopped in front of the cave entrance. Leaving the engine idling, the driver dismounted and disappeared inside. A minute later, he reappeared and began searching the area.

"What's he looking for?" Kate whispered to Rand.

"I think the better question is, what did he find?"

Chills skittered up her spine. Even from a distance, and with their view partially obscured, the man appeared large and menacing. The pelting rain had no effect on his aggressive prowl as he inspected the area.

"He's found our footprints and the hoofprints," Rand said.

"What will he do?"

The question was ans_____
next shallow breath. T_____
she swore, stared dire_____

Cathy McDavid is truly blessed to have been penning Westerns and small-town stories for Harlequin since 2005. With over fifty titles in print and 1.6 million-plus books sold, Cathy is also a member of the prestigious Romance Writers of America's Honor Roll. This "almost" Arizona native and mother of grown twins is married to her own real-life sweetheart. After leaving the corporate world seven years ago, she now spends her days penning stories about good-looking cowboys riding the range, busting broncs and sweeping gals off their feet— oops, no. Make that, winning the hearts of feisty, independent women who give the cowboys a run for their money. It's a tough job, but she's willing to make the sacrifice.

Books by Cathy McDavid

Love Inspired Mountain Rescue

Wildfire Threat
Blizzard Refuge

Visit the Author Profile page at Harlequin.com.

Mountain Storm Survival

CATHY McDAVID

LOVE INSPIRED

INSPIRATIONAL ROMANCE

ISBN-13: 978-1-335-46847-5

Mountain Storm Survival

For questions and comments about the quality of this book, please contact us at CustomerService@Harlequin.com.

Love Inspired
22 Adelaide St. West, 41st Floor
Toronto, Ontario M5H 4E3, Canada
www.LoveInspired.com

Printed in U.S.A.

Recycling programs for this product may not exist in your area.

For if ye forgive men their trespasses,
your heavenly Father will also forgive you.
—*Matthew* 6:14

To my incredible, amazing, talented daughter.
You never cease to amaze me with your many
accomplishments or charm me with your zest for life.
Here's to more adventures together.
My bags are packed.

Chapter One

A high-pitched whinny pierced the air, blood chilling in its fury and terror. Something had upset Goliath, Still Water Ranch's prize palomino stallion. A loud crack followed, then another—steel horseshoes against wood fencing. When the horse got like this, property damage was the least of Rand Walkins's concerns. Someone could get injured. Badly.

He tossed a fifty-pound bale of hay from the stack onto the flatbed trailer parked beside the feed barn. "Wait here," he instructed his young helper, a sixth grader attending the Youth Wrangler Camp.

"What was that?" the boy asked, his baggy basketball shorts and athletic shoes out of place on the forty-acre horse ranch.

Rand ignored the question. Instead, he half jogged, half hobbled across the long open stretch of hard ground to the paddock where Goliath had been turned out for the day. With each step, pain seized his damaged legs, but he kept going.

The scene that greeted him had him clamping his teeth together in frustration. Two girls, campers the same age as his young helper, were with Goliath. The brown-haired one straddled the fence. Her companion, taller and skinny enough to get lost behind a fence post, was in the paddock. Ignoring Goliath's fit of rage and the potential danger she was in, she approached the stallion with raised arms in what Rand guessed was an attempt to pet him.

"Easy, boy," she cooed. "It's okay."

Rand slowed to a stop. Sweat soaked his shirt collar, and his lungs labored to draw sufficient air. Not from exertion but the cramps that attacked his legs with their razor-sharp claws.

"Get out of there," he hollered, his voice choppy.

Both girls turned to face him, their expressions startled at first, then defiant in the way kids doubled down when caught doing something wrong.

"I'm not hurtin' him," the skinny girl said.

"That's not the problem. He's going to hurt *you*." Rand approached the paddock gate, each step an agony. He hated appearing weak, so he forced himself not to limp. "Now back up slowly. Then walk, not run, to the gate."

She raised her chin.

"Do it, or I'm sending you home today. You know the rules." He fired a stern look at her friend on the fence. This one showed some sense and immediately scampered down.

Goliath stomped his heavy foot, stirring up a small cloud of dust. By this time, a crowd had gathered that included more of the Youth Wrangler Camp members, old Bill Nault, who everyone called Grandpa Billy and Ansel Laurent, owner of Still Water Ranch. A pair of black-and-white border collies sat at Ansel's heels, their tongues lolling and their wagging tails sweeping the ground.

Everyone, dogs included, watched the goings-on with interest. Ansel frowned. Grandpa Billy, however, wore the patient look of someone who'd seen this before and wasn't terribly worried.

Rand slid the latch and opened the gate just wide enough to slip inside the paddock. Goliath eyed the intruders in his domain and stomped his foot again. A foot that had felled grown men and could easily launch a hundred-pound preteen into orbit.

"Get a move on," Ansel called to the girl. "Rest assured, you don't want me to be the one coming in there after you."

"Okay, okay." She inched toward the gate, her back to the paddock fence.

When she got within arm's length, Rand grabbed hold of her and dragged her the remaining distance.

"Hey," she yelled when he propelled her through the gate. "Quit it."

Lord, grant me patience and understanding, he silently prayed and hurried out after her, shutting the gate behind him.

Goliath whinnied again, this time in triumph. Rearing on his hind legs, he pawed the air before dropping to the ground. The early afternoon sun gleamed off his golden hide as he pranced in circles, head held high, mane and tail floating on the breeze. He was a magnificent sight and king of all he surveyed.

Rand envied the horse's athleticism. He'd once been like that. Strong and powerful with legs that could carry him for miles. But that was another lifetime. Before the accident.

"Cool," said one of the boys. Given the way his gaze followed Goliath, he was referring to the horse and not the girls' antics.

Good. Hopefully, he wasn't a troublemaker like these two.

Ansel believed God had called on him to help underprivileged youths by hosting a twice-yearly camp. Most of the sixth-graders who attended had never seen a horse up close, much less ridden one. They were required to perform chores, attend chapel and Bible study, take part in group sessions and obey the rules. In exchange, they got to enjoy the many fun activities.

The majority of kids left with a confidence and self-esteem they hadn't previously possessed, and a few with a desire to continue attending church. If the camp made a difference in even one kid's life, turned them away from the wrong path, Ansel considered it a success.

"Get to the kitchen," the ranch owner told the girls. "You're both on cleanup duty for the rest of the day."

"Cleanup duty? Not fair," the taller one protested. "We didn't do anything—"

"Stop right there," he said. "You used up your one and only strike when you climbed in that paddock. If you want to stay, I suggest you toe the line." He pointed in the direction of the ranch house, a good quarter mile up the dirt road. "I'll call ahead and let Mrs. Sciacca know you're on your way."

"It's hot," she complained.

And humid. Arizona's monsoon season had arrived early to the Superstition Mountains, appearing in late June rather than July. Still Water Ranch sat at the base of the mountains and bordered federal land. Flash floods from runoffs were problematic during monsoon season, stranding area residents as well as causing significant destruction to land and homes.

"No hotter than it was in the paddock when you were pestering poor Goliath," Ansel told the girls.

The taller one huffed in annoyance. She clasped her friend's hand, and together they trudged off toward the house.

Maybe they'd think about the wisdom of their choices during the short walk. That was Ansel's plan, Rand knew, though it may not work with the tall girl. She seemed intent on testing boundaries.

Rand had been a little like her as a teenager, thinking he was invincible and smarter than everyone around him. Then he'd been humbled. Nothing like hearing a doctor's grim prognosis to change a person's attitude. Rand had been angry at first. Then, grateful when he took that first unaided step. With it, he welcomed God into his life, knowing without a doubt it was only because of His grace that Rand recovered enough to lead a fulfilling life.

Mostly. He'd never compete on the rodeo circuit again. Never ride a bull or a bronc or wrestle calves. Never win the world championship title that had been his dream. But he could hold down a job and walk into church every Sunday. Dance with his mother at his sister's wedding. That was something. A big something.

"Everybody, back to work," Ansel said and motioned with his hand.

The dogs jumped up and, for no reason other than they were young and full of energy, began to play fight with each other. The camp members wandered off to resume cleaning stalls in the mare barn or packing for the overnight trail ride leaving in the morning.

Grandpa Billy chuckled to himself. "Gonna have your hands full with those two on the ride tomorrow."

"Don't remind me." Rand shook his head. His breathing had returned to normal as the pain in his legs receded. Though, by tonight, he'd be paying the price for his little jaunt and need an extra round of PT exercises.

"Speaking of which," Ansel said. "Can you spare a few minutes, Rand?"

"Sure thing, boss."

"I'll check on the farrier. He should be about finished shoeing those horses." Grandpa Billy excused himself and, whistling for the dogs, headed toward the corral housing the ranch's working horses. It was separated from Goliath's private residence by a state-of-the-art mare barn and a stable with two-dozen prime cutting horses in various stages of training.

Ansel tilted his head. "Walk with me." As he and Rand strolled toward the ranch office, Ansel phoned the cook and told her the girls were on their way there and why. When he finished, he disconnected and addressed Rand. "I have news."

"I'm hoping you hired a new hand."

"I did."

"Glad to hear." Otherwise, they'd be shorthanded on the trail ride. These kids were inexperienced, and they'd need at least one wrangler for every three of them.

Ansel stroked his salt-and-pepper beard, a habit when he was weighing a decision or carefully choosing his words. "She's arriving shortly."

"She?" Rand asked.

"Don't be looking like that. We've had some capable women wranglers here at Still Water. One who taught you a thing or two when you first hired on, as I recall."

"That's true."

"This one's experienced. Comes highly recommended. And—" Ansel paused "—she needs a break."

Of course she did. That was Ansel's way. Hadn't he given Rand a break when he'd needed one?

"I believe there's a reason she was led here."

Rand smiled. "That can be said for most of us."

"She's special, though. Different. I want you to get along with her. It's important. To her, and I think it might be important to you, too."

"Why wouldn't I get along with her?"

Ansel stroked his beard again. "She's someone from your past."

Rand searched his memory and came up blank. He got along well with everyone, including the few women he'd dated through the years. They'd all parted on civil, if not good, terms.

"You say from my past like she and I have bad blood."

"You know I'm not one to interfere in your life," Ansel said. "Advise you or mentor you, sure. But how you live yours is your choice. When I spoke to this gal and heard her story, I was genuinely moved. This is a chance for you to fully heal and find peace. You need that, even if you won't admit it."

Rand was getting frustrated. "I've healed, Ansel."

"Have you?"

Rand's answer was cut short by the sound of tires crunching on the dirt road; the two of them turned to see a dented and rust-eaten pickup heading straight for them. The driver glanced their way and then parked in front of the ranch office. The door creaked as it opened and a cowgirl hopped out, her jeans worn, her hat weathered, her boots scruffy and her thick brown hair falling to midback.

Recognition hit Rand like the shock from a live wire. *No, not her!*

She nodded in greeting and walked toward them, shoulders squared in an obvious brave front but trepidation lighting her eyes. Rand knew they were a deep hazel. He'd never forget the day, over ten years ago, when she'd flashed those eyes at him and smiled beguilingly.

Anger raged inside him, growing until it filled his chest and strangled his throat. He squeezed his eyes shut and, in his mind, relived the fall in nightmarish detail. He couldn't stop his hands from shaking.

"Easy, son," Ansel said, attempting to calm Rand as he had many times before. "You're all right."

No, he wasn't. "Anybody else but her, boss."

That was a lie. Anybody but her and her three accomplices.

Ansel was right. Rand hadn't healed. Try as he might, hard as he prayed, he'd never been able to forgive them for what they'd done, and he never would.

Kate Spencer had prayed daily for an opportunity to apologize to Rand for her part in the tragedy that nearly cost him the ability to walk. Now that the moment was here, she wanted only to turn tail and flee.

He hated her. It shone in the rigid set of his jaw and the sparks shooting from his eyes. All right, maybe *hate* was too strong a word. But he wished her gone from Still Water Ranch, and was clearly in no mood for an apology.

Ansel had been wrong. Why had she pleaded her

case to him? She shouldn't have taken the job he offered. Shouldn't have put her hope for absolution above Rand's need for a life free from emotional strife caused by her presence.

She stopped and waited, unsure of what to do next.

"Give her a chance, son," Ansel said. He put his hand on Rand's shoulder. "This is hard for her, too."

Rand snorted. With disgust? Disbelief? Anger?

"She's paid the price for what she did, and then some," Ansel added.

Almost six years in prison. Her original sentence had been twenty-two months, but Kate had made mistakes. Stupid mistakes that had added to her sentence.

"It's time for both of you to put the past behind you," Ansel said. "You can't change what happened. You can only grow from it."

Rand stiffened.

Kate swallowed. Neither of them had yet to speak.

He'd grown taller since high school. Six feet, give or take. The top half of him had filled out. Wide shoulders. Strong arms. By comparison, his legs weren't exactly straight and, she noticed, were bent at slightly different angles.

How extensive were his limitations? He could walk, clearly. And he couldn't hold down a job as manager of the largest cutting horse ranch in Arizona without being able to ride, reasonably well at least.

Thank You, Lord, for that.

His pale blond hair was cut shorter, but his intelligent brown eyes were the same. They noticed everything, and, right now, they studied her scruffy appearance.

Kate lifted her chin a fraction. Employment wasn't easy to come by for former inmates. She had no spare money for nice clothes or a fancy vehicle. If people were going to judge her for that, and not what lay in her heart, then so be it.

"Rand," she started. "I'm so sor—"

He didn't let her finish and stormed off, his gait awkward and stilted, yet proud. She clenched her teeth to stop herself from crying. Tears were a sign of weakness.

"That didn't go well," she said to Ansel.

"Give him time."

"This is a bad idea."

"This is a good idea. It just got off to a bad start."

She blew out a breath. "I think I should go."

"Let me show you around instead." He gestured for Kate to accompany him.

She did. Reluctantly. A tour wouldn't hurt anything, and the ranch owner had been kind to her. She could always leave afterward.

"Gary with the employment assistance agency told me about you for a reason, Kate. And not just because I'm shorthanded and in need of a wrangler. God has a plan and brought you to Still Water Ranch. I think it's for you and Rand to unburden yourselves. You're seeking absolution. He needs to forgive. This is your opportunity and his."

"I don't know about that," she said. "Rand's angry at me, and with good reason. He lost his career after the fall. His entire life."

"And he found a new one, a life he loves. Guess he forgets that every once in a while. Being blindsided today didn't help. My fault. I should have warned him."

"Mr. Laurent—"

"I told you to call me Ansel."

"Ansel. You're very nice and generous, but I probably should refuse the job. I don't want to cause trouble."

"What do you say to a trial period? If after the end of youth camp you still want to leave, I won't stop you."

"Can I avoid Rand?"

He chuckled. "You're going to cross paths with him. It's unavoidable."

Indecision tore at Kate. A week's wages, a roof over her head and three squares a day would be more than she had yesterday. It would give her time to regroup and look for another job in the evenings.

But to what end? She'd submit a bunch of applications that would be rejected, like always. Subject herself to an emotional beating in more ways than one. Rand, too. Was that what she wanted?

Her stomach growled, and her back pinched from sleeping in her truck the last two nights.

"Okay. I accept."

"Good." Ansel smiled. "Now, about that tour. Over there are the arenas. The larger one's for competitions and events and the smaller one's for practice. Behind the mare barn and stables is the pasture for our brood mares and their foals. Another one houses the yearlings."

He explained the ranch's breeding, raising and training operation as he introduced her to Goliath. The handsome resident stallion seemed to instantly size Kate up with his intelligent eyes. Across from the stables stood a grain shed and covered haystacks. In the distant pasture, Rand drove a tractor hauling a flatbed trailer loaded with hay bales. A boy sat on the trailer, his legs dangling over the side. At least two-dozen horses plodded along behind them as the tractor made its way to one of the metal feeders on the south end of the pasture.

"That youngster is with the youth camp I was telling you about," Ansel said.

They stopped along the pasture fence to watch Rand and the boy feed the horses.

"Youth Wrangler Camp lasts nine days," he continued. "The participants work hard while they're here. It's not all fun and games, though there is plenty of that, too. As long as they obey the rules, do their chores without complaint, attend church service and Bible study, and participate in group counseling sessions, they get to enjoy the activities."

"What kind of activities?" Kate asked.

"Riding lessons. Campfires and cookouts. Movie night. Their last full day, we have a tournament. Races and games, mostly on horseback."

"Sounds great."

"It's one of the highlights. That, and the overnight trail ride, which leaves bright and early tomorrow morning. You'll be going along. One of four wranglers."

"What are my other duties?"

"I'll give you the lowdown on the way to the bunkhouse." They started walking again.

"Do I report to Rand?"

"You'll report to Marcos. He's the head wrangler. I'll introduce you to him later. He reports to Rand, who's ranch manager."

"Gotcha."

"My advice is to keep your head down and your nose to the grindstone."

"Yes, sir."

"Most of your job will be overseeing the equipment. Repairs, cleaning, making sure the saddlebags are fully stocked. Then there's running to town for supplies and medicine. Bathing and grooming and exercising the horses. If there's any grunt work to be done, you'll be the one assigned to it."

They came upon a pair of small, quaint buildings opposite the mare barn that resembled cabins out of an Old West TV show. A circular firepit with an iron cooking grill sat in front of them, with a stack of neatly cut wood nearby. A couple dozen weathered lawn chairs surrounded the firepit, waiting for their nightly occupants.

"Bunkhouse on the right is for the men," Ansel said. "One on the left is for the women. You'll find a vacant bunk inside. Cots and sleeping bags have been set up in the middle for the girl youth camp participants. You'll have to crawl over them, but it's only temporary."

"I don't mind."

"Mrs. Sciacca, the ranch cook, delivers breakfast burritos promptly at five thirty every morning outside the office, along with a brown bag lunch you can take with you for wherever you'll be during the day. Dinner is at five thirty every evening around the campfire. Usually stew or chili or goulash. Something simple and filling. If you don't like the food, you can fix your own. The bunkhouse has a fridge and a microwave."

Was he kidding? After prison fare, Kate was hardly picky. "It sounds delicious."

"You get paid every Friday at four. My wife can answer any questions regarding payroll."

Kate would have to make the paltry balance in her checking account last.

"Need help unloading your stuff?"

"No, sir. I've got it." She didn't have much.

"Bible study is after dinner tonight. If you're interested."

"I am."

"Rand will be there."

What was her new boss expecting her to say? Kate wasn't sure. After a moment, she blurted, "I heard how you and the Cowboy Church helped him find God."

Ansel's brows rose. "Kept tabs on him, did you?"

"Not me. Someone I know."

"Family?"

"No. I don't hear much from them."

Truthfully, Kate's parents and sister hadn't spoken to her since her sentencing hearing. They were ashamed and told people she wanted nothing to do with them rather than the truth: they wanted nothing to do with her. At least her brother sent her the occasional email, which she answered.

"An old classmate from high school has stayed in touch with me," Kate said.

Ansel nodded. "Well, we didn't help Rand find God. He did that himself. We were just there to support him."

"That's not what my classmate told me."

"Oh?"

"She said Rand met you and the members of Cowboy Church on the junior rodeo circuit. Not being a regular churchgoer, he didn't have much use for you at first. But after the accident, you and the members came to the hospital and stayed in the waiting room for over a week, taking shifts. You prayed for his recovery and that he'd be able to walk again even when the doctors predicted he wouldn't."

Kate knew that part for a fact. One of the reasons the judge had thrown the book at her and the other three involved was the gravity of Rand's injury and likelihood he'd be in a wheelchair for the rest of his life.

"When the surgery went better than expected," she continued, "and Rand was able to stand, he invited you and the other church members into his room, where you all prayed together."

Ansel smiled as if she'd stirred pleasant memories.

"You made a lot of trips to visit him after that, at the hospital and his parents' house," she continued. "Cheered his successes. Encouraged him when he was down. And after his second surgery when he took his first step, he made a commitment to God and the Cowboy Church."

"He was blessed by our Lord's good grace and a determination like no one I've ever met before."

She knew the whole story. Two more surgeries followed. By then, Rand was attending Northern Arizona University. He eventually graduated with a degree in equine management. Diploma in hand, he hired on at Still Water Ranch where he was eventually promoted to manager.

About that time, Kate was up for parole.

"I'm very glad." She lowered her gaze. "It doesn't make what I did okay. I'm not saying that. I just would hate for him to suffer more than he has already."

"Or you, young lady."

She drew back. "I'm fine."

"Gary told me you've been through a lot."

"Not like Rand," she said with a finality to let Ansel know she'd rather not talk about her six years in prison or the four that had followed.

Ansel nodded, getting the message. "Why don't you unpack and then meet me in the office. There's some paperwork you need to complete. I'll call Marcos and have him meet us there. He can get you started on organizing the equipment for tomorrow's trail ride."

"Yes, sir."

"Park your truck behind the grain shed with the rest of the ranch vehicles."

"Will do."

Kate hurried to her pickup, then moved it as instructed. She had little to unload and would only need to make one trip to the bunkhouse. Since her release, she'd gone from job to job, town to town, never staying long. Sometimes the decision was hers, other times, she was asked to leave. Former convicts tended to make people ill at ease.

At the door to the bunkhouse, she knocked. When no one answered, she tried the knob, found the door unlocked and went inside. One of the six beds lined against the wall appeared to be unoccupied. Kate didn't wonder about her bunkmates. She'd spent years sharing communal space with other women and knew how to keep to herself and get along. Zigzagging through the obstacle course of six cots crammed into the small living room area, she reached the empty bed and dropped her duffel bag and backpack onto it.

At the foot of every bed sat a metal chest with a small padlock. Hers was the only one with a key in the lock. Good. Kate transferred her few valuables from her duffel to her backpack, preferring not to leave them out where they might tempt sticky fingers. It was a habit formed from necessity. She'd been the victim of theft before, both in prison and after her release.

She locked her backpack inside the chest and added the small silver key to her key ring—which she stuffed in her pocket before heading to the office to meet Ansel.

She passed a black horse tied to the hitching rail and paused at the office door, which was open a crack.

"Hello," Kate said, and slowly entered.

A tall cowboy stood in the middle of the room. He wore a pale brown shirt with sleeves rolled up to the elbows. She'd seen that shirt a short while ago.

Rand!

At the sound of her voice, he turned and narrowed his gaze at her.

Startled, she retreated a step and stuttered. "S-sorry. Ansel said to m-meet him here."

"He had an emergency. I'll handle your paperwork and get you started."

Her heart banged like a bass drum. "What about Marcos?"

"He rode up the north trail for a look around. We got reports of a mountain lion sighting this morning."

"Mountain lion! Are the foals safe?"

"It's nothing to worry about. Not yet. If there is a mountain lion hanging around, he likely won't stay. They don't much like civilization."

Huh. Here they were, she and Rand, having a normal work conversation. Was it possible he'd just needed to get used to the idea of her being at Still Water Ranch?

He picked up a clipboard from the desk and handed it to her. "These are the employment documents. Go ahead and fill them out. I'll need two forms of ID. I assume you have them?"

His former civil tone had been replaced with one on the brusque side of surly. So much for him just needing to get used to the idea.

"Yes." She patted her shirt pocket.

"A phone? You'll need one."

She pulled it out and showed him on the chance he didn't believe her.

He gave the pay-by-the-minute, bottom-of-the-line

model a passing glance. "I'll be back in ten. You should be finished by then."

He left, not quite slamming the door behind him. No subtleties there. He was unhappy about being put in charge of her and had telegraphed that to her loud and clear.

Much as she wanted to, Kate didn't cringe.

One week. She could do this. Then, as she drove away with Still Water Ranch in her rearview mirror, she could tell herself she'd tried her best.

Chapter Two

Grandpa Billy ambled over to where Rand and Mega Max stood outside the office. Rand brushed the stout black, his ranch horse of choice, with a stainless steel currycomb.

"Hey there, partner. You plan on grooming that horse right down to his bare hide?"

Rand stuffed the currycomb into his back jeans pocket and gave the horse's neck a pat.

"Let me guess," Grandpa Billy said. "That pretty gal in the office there has you tied in knots."

"You've been at Still Water longer than anyone else. Tell me—why did Ansel hire her?"

"You know why."

Rand fought to control his temper. "How I deal with my past isn't any of his business."

Grandpa Billy chuckled. "Or not deal with it."

Rand bristled. "I said I'd cover for Marcos and get Kate started on the saddlebags for the trail ride. What else does Ansel want from me?"

"Look, partner, I agree. The boss shouldn't have brought her here without talking to you first."

"You agree?" Rand drew back to study the older man. "Really?"

"But sometimes God works through others when we—"

"Need help. I get it."

"When we're too stubborn for our own good," Grandpa Billy corrected him. "There's a corner of your heart that's rock-hard. You can't let love in or hate out. Until you do something different, that will never change."

That was probably what Ansel had been thinking when he agreed to let Kate come to Still Water Ranch.

"What if I don't want to change?" Rand said.

"Well, that's your decision. All Ansel's done is give you an opportunity."

The anger Rand had felt earlier rose again to wrap its fists around his throat. "Because of her, I lost my rodeo career and live with chronic pain. I almost didn't walk again."

"That prank wasn't her idea. Them boys used her as a way to distract you while they did their dirty deed. She was a victim, just like you."

"Not like me. And no one forced her. She could have refused."

"True enough, I suppose. But she was mighty young and naive. She deserves to be cut a little slack."

Rand wasn't convinced. He'd sat in that courtroom and listened to Kate testify. Watched her face as the words poured from her. She'd known what she was doing and willingly agreed to it.

"She paid a dear price," Grandpa Billy said. "A far bigger price than them boys whose idea it was and who cut those straps on your saddle. They were out of prison and roaming the streets—what, three years later? Paroled early because of overcrowding and got to go on with their lives. Seems to me you should be mad at them more'n you are Kate."

"I am mad at them."

"Not as much. Mind telling me what happened? How'd she hurt you, Rand?"

He slowed his breathing, centered himself and silently counted. It was one of the techniques he'd learned in therapy to treat his PTSD. He didn't like thinking of himself as someone with an emotional affliction on top of a physical one. But no one survived what he had and came away unscathed.

"She should be finished by now," he said. "I'm going to head inside."

"Go easy on her."

"I'll try."

Grandpa Billy ambled off. At the door, Rand stomped his boots to dislodge the dirt and let Kate know he was back. Turning the knob, he entered the office.

She glanced at him from where she occupied the visitor chair.

"All done?" he asked.

In response, she held up the clipboard.

He took it and reviewed the paperwork. Everything appeared to be filled out correctly. "I need to see your two forms of ID before I can sign off."

She passed him her driver's license and social security card. He examined them closely and checked them against the top two pages.

"They're legit," she said.

Without a word, he returned the IDs and signed off. He noticed she'd listed a bank account for direct deposit of wages. Some of the short-term employees who found their way to Still Water Ranch preferred to use those check-cashing places. Was Kate more responsible? Did she intend to stay in the area?

Grandpa Billy had been right when he said the boys were the masterminds behind the accident. As the prosecutor had explained to Rand, the two felonies she'd committed were of the lower-class variety. Plus, she'd fully cooperated with the authorities, confessing the entire story. While the judge had thrown the book at her cohorts, he'd gone a little easier on Kate. According to what the prosecutor had told him, it was in prison when the real trouble had started.

Grandpa Billy had also been right about Kate hurting Rand. Not that he'd admit it.

"Everything seems in order." He set the clipboard on the desk for Ansel's wife. She handled the payroll and bookkeeping for the ranch. "This way to the tack shed."

Outside, he and Kate passed several of the youth camp members on their walk to the horse stables. Behind the building was a large structure with a steep roof. It contained the ranch's extensive inventory of tack and riding equipment.

"Wow," Kate exclaimed when they entered, her eyes wide. "This is incredible."

Rand surveyed the racks holding dozens of saddles in all makes and sizes, picturing them from her perspective. Granted, there were a lot.

His gaze roamed the rows and rows of bridles hanging from hooks in the walls and a pair of free-standing shelves holding every kind of bit imaginable. Halters, martingales, curb straps, lunge lines and horse blankets rounded out the equipment. Three floor-to-ceiling cabinets contained enough cleaning supplies and medical products to fill a small store.

He could understand why someone in Kate's circumstances would be impressed. She'd neither come from money nor had she traveled in the same circles as her older, more accomplished sister, a champion barrel racer. The same circles Rand had traveled in.

"We have a dozen kids going on the overnight trail ride tomorrow," he said. "They're each going to need a fully stocked saddlebag." He tilted his head at a pile of canvas saddlebags in the corner, all weathered and worn and with a hundred stories to tell. "What's your phone number? I'll text you the list. You'll find everything you need here to stock the bags."

She recited her number. While he typed a message to her, she explored the building, familiarizing herself with the contents. A few minutes later, he hit Send. Her phone buzzed, and she opened the text message.

"Any questions?" he asked.

She read her phone screen. "I don't think so."

"Okay. I'm outta here, then. Remember to distribute the weight evenly on each side. If you have any problems or can't find something, text me. Otherwise, I'll see you in an hour."

"Wait. Do I pack saddlebags for the wranglers?"

"No, just the kids. We have our own."

"What, um, about me?"

"Right." He'd forgotten to include her. "Pack one for yourself."

"Can I take personal items along on the ride?"

He couldn't stay a second longer. He had to get out. "As long as they don't weigh over five pounds. You have equipment and supplies to carry, too."

"Got it."

He left, trying hard to maintain a sedate pace and not appear as if he was desperate to escape her presence.

Thankfully, Marcos returned not long after that. The head wrangler took over supervising Kate and monitoring her progress, leaving Rand in charge of the riding lesson for the camp members. None of the dozen preteens had ever ridden before arriving two days ago. The experienced and docile horses made learning easy and fun.

"Joey, relax your hold on the reins," Rand called out. "The horse can tell if you're nervous. Aiesha, no trotting. Make her walk. Remember, you're in charge."

The jovial girl laughed. "I'm not in charge, Mr. Rand."

"Yes, you are."

He stood in the center of the small arena as the riders circled around him, taking direction and practicing for the trail ride.

The girl who'd broken the rules and climbed into Goliath's paddock earlier that day passed by him. A review of the camp admission forms had refreshed his memory. Her name was Serene. A contradiction, as far as he was concerned. She more resembled the fierce storms that rolled in from the desert this time of year. The other girl—Brielle, she went by Brie—was her foster sister. They lived with the same family and, according to the notes, were inseparable. They'd also been in some minor trouble at home and school.

He'd be wise to keep an eye on them. As if he didn't already have enough on his plate with Kate.

After the lesson, he supervised the unsaddling and unbridling of the horses and insured they were sufficiently cooled down before being retired to the corral.

During the trail ride, each kid would be responsible for all aspects of their horse's care and their own equipment. They were also expected to contribute to any camp chores.

By the time the kids were done with their horses, it was close to five thirty. Everyone returned to the bunkhouse to freshen up before dinner. Rand combed his hair, changed into a fresh shirt and grabbed his Bible.

He stepped outside, immediately searching for Kate. There was no sign of her. Surely, she wouldn't miss dinner in an attempt to avoid him.

Kids milled about, hungry and ready to chow down on the chicken and dumplings simmering in the large pot sitting atop the grill. A few had already claimed a chair by the fire.

Mrs. Sciacca, a short, wide, middle-aged woman with zero patience for shenanigans and a hugely generous heart, tended the food. Serene and Brie, as part of their kitchen duty, set out bowls, spoons, cups and napkins on a six-foot folding table. At the end of the table sat three tall jugs with spigots, containing iced tea, fruit punch and water. A large enamel coffeepot perched on the grill beside the pot of chicken and dumplings.

Ansel helped his wife to an empty chair. Rand hadn't asked about the emergency that had taken his boss away from the ranch. If Ansel wanted Rand to know, he'd say something. Rand suspected it had to do with Ansel's grandson, who was scheduled for yet another surgery to repair a congenital heart defect. Rand murmured a prayer under his breath, asking God to watch over the boy and his family during this difficult time.

Just as Mrs. Sciacca hollered, "Dinner's served," the women's bunkhouse door opened, and Kate emerged.

She nodded and smiled shyly but didn't talk to anyone and avoided Rand. That suited him just fine. He was inclined to avoid her, too.

They sat on opposite sides of the campfire and ate. Rand didn't converse much, either, other than a word here and there. He was too busy trying not to look like he was watching Kate's every move.

She ate a lot for a slender gal. And fast, shoveling spoonful after spoonful of chicken and dumplings into her mouth. Why? Was she afraid if she didn't finish quickly, someone would take her dinner away? Did that happen in prison? She practically inhaled the ice-cream sandwich for dessert.

"You want another one?" CeCe asked. She worked for Ansel's wife as a housekeeper's assistant.

Kate shook her head. "Thanks anyway."

"You sure? There are plenty. We can have all we want."

"Seriously?"

CeCe chuckled. "Go on."

Kate reached into the cooler and withdrew a second ice-cream sandwich. Slowly, as if unveiling a treasure, she unwrapped the frozen treat and bit off a corner. A minute later, she'd devoured the entire thing. Her cheeks flushed a bright red, and she turned away in embarrassment.

Even as Rand wondered what she'd gone through that caused her to eat like a stray dog living on the streets, he wished he wasn't curious about her.

When dinner was over, Mrs. Sciacca and the foster sisters cleaned up. With the trash and leftovers loaded in the back of Mrs. Sciacca's SUV, she drove back to the ranch house and Bible study began, led by Ansel.

Rand expected Kate to return to the bunkhouse. Not

only did she remain in her seat, she withdrew a small, tattered Bible from inside her shirt. She turned it over in her hands with a familiarity that bespoke a close, personal relationship with the words written inside.

He couldn't have been more surprised. This woman, the one refusing to meet his gaze from across the campfire, was a devout Christian?

Impossible.

At least, the version of Kate he'd carried in his mind since the accident wasn't a Christian. Otherwise, she couldn't have done to him what she had.

A blanket of iron-gray clouds obscured the moon and all but a few stars. If not for the campfire and the exterior lights on the bunkhouses, those at the Bible study would have been cast in complete darkness.

"Was that a raindrop?" CeCe wiped her forearm.

Kate peered at the sky as if it could answer her bunkmate's question. "It's not supposed to rain until tomorrow and then there's only a fifty percent chance."

"Hope you don't have any problems on the trail ride."

Kate liked CeCe. She'd learned to read people quickly and trust her instincts. With her plump cheeks and charmingly crooked front teeth, CeCe was who and what she appeared to be: straightforward, hardworking and good-natured.

"I suppose we can always turn around and come home."

"Maybe," CeCe mused. "Or not. Ansel believes we all face hardships and shouldn't quit at the first sign of trouble. Sticking it out builds character."

"Does trouble include thunder and lightning?"

"A storm is different. But if we're talking about a

light shower…" She shrugged. "You packed waterproof ponchos for everyone, right?"

"I did." Kate glanced at the sky again.

She'd slept in her truck often enough while the rain poured. Beneath the shelter of a tent and inside a warm sleeping bag would be no worse, despite lying on the rocky ground.

"I enjoyed Bible study," she said, changing the subject. "The story of Ruth is one of my favorites."

CeCe nodded. "Ansel is a fine teacher. Wait until you hear him talk at Sunday service. He has a mighty gift."

Kate and CeCe had decided to stay after everyone left and enjoy a cup of herbal tea around the campfire before retiring. It was only eight o'clock, and Kate was too agitated after the day's events to sleep.

"I heard he's a founding member of the Saguaro Cowboy Church," Kate said.

"He is. He joined as a young man when he first started competing and still attends rodeos, bringing the word of God. That's where he met Rand."

Made sense. And would explain Ansel's visits to the hospital and his dedication to Rand's recovery.

"Did you also meet Ansel through the church?" CeCe asked.

Kate considered how much to admit. She'd learned the hard way that people were often uncomfortable around former felons. Others pretended not to be but secretly fidgeted and fretted. A few, like Ansel, were willing to look past her history and accept her as the person she was today. Others were convinced she was the same rotten-to-the-core person now as then. Like her parents and sister. And Rand.

"Actually, I was referred to him by a job service company."

"Cool." CeCe smiled.

Kate bolstered her nerve. The news about her would get out sooner or later. She'd rather it come from her. "A job service company that helps former felons find employment."

CeCe gave Kate a lingering look as realization dawned. "Ah. Okay."

"I served six years. Should have been twenty-two months. Less with good behavior. I had trouble adjusting to prison life at first. Made some wrong decisions."

"You don't have to talk about this if you don't want to. But if you do, I'm a good listener."

CeCe's tone held no judgment or disapproval—which was a rarity. Kate hadn't planned on revealing more. She found herself reconsidering.

"About four years into my extended sentence," she continued, "I was beaten during a…an altercation." A turf war, but no need to mention that. "I met a woman in the infirmary. She attended a twice-weekly worship service in the prison chapel and told me about her beliefs."

Kate had had no choice but to listen, due to her restraints. At first, she'd scoffed at what the woman said, even going so far as to sling insults at her. But eventually, the woman's words breached Kate's barriers, and she'd started to cry. Huge, wracking sobs as if a dam had been released.

"She invited me to attend the next worship service. I turned her down. But the following Sunday, I poked my head in the chapel door."

CeCe leaned forward. "What happened?"

"I was welcomed, and I stayed. I never missed a service after that."

It took a while for Kate to dedicate her life to God. She'd had a lot of questions and doubts and didn't believe herself worthy. She couldn't imagine God forgiving her, much less loving her. He had, however. To this day, she could remember the elation that had washed over her when she accepted God into her heart.

"Cool." CeCe smiled. "What was her name? The woman from the infirmary?"

"Rosario. We stay in touch."

"That's nice." CeCe sipped her tea. She didn't pressure Kate to continue, letting her reveal as much or as little as she wanted in her own time.

"Prison was a nightmare," Kate said after a moment. "I got in trouble for fighting my first week. The inmates pegged me as easy pickings and stole my food. I was starving. On the fifth day, I fought back—which earned me a trip to the hole for a week."

While difficult and frightening, solitary confinement had also been a relief. Food restored Kate physically and freedom from her tormenters gave her time to think and plan.

"But that wasn't your fault," CeCe said. "You were just defending yourself."

"Doesn't matter. I learned pretty quickly there's only one way to survive in prison, and that's safety in numbers. Problem was, I chose to join one of the more violent gangs. I did acquire a lot of skills. I also added years to my sentence. For fighting and once for attacking a guard. Rosario changed my life. Because of her, I was able to get paroled."

"And because of your faith."

Kate nodded, her attention drawn to a movement near the stables. The next second, whatever had been there vanished. Probably a cat on the hunt for mice.

CeCe stood and, using a nearby shovel left for just that purpose, moved the coals away from the firepit's edges and toward the center where they would slowly burn down.

"I'd never been in trouble before," Kate said, watching her. "Not even shoplifting or trespassing. Too busy competing in barrel racing. I wasn't very good." Not like her older, prettier, more talented sister who'd won a state championship and was reigning rodeo queen. "I had a crush on this boy. And I wanted him to ask me out." She exhaled a long breath. "It sounds incredibly stupid now, but I was in high school."

"Hey." CeCe replaced the shovel and sat back down. "Been there, done that."

"I should have known something wasn't right. He barely ever looked at me, much less spoke to me. This one Saturday we were at the Gold Rush Rodeo, and, out of the blue, he approached me with two of his pals and invited me to the prom. The prom!"

"That's awesome."

"Well, there was a catch. I had to distract his rival for ten minutes so the boy and his pals could, as he put it, play a practical joke on him."

"What?" CeCe frowned.

"Yeah. I should have refused. Instead, I took what the boy said at face value because he was popular and had these dimples, and I liked him."

"I'm guessing the practical joke went wrong."

"Very wrong."

Kate noticed the movement again, this time closer. That cat was sure intent on reducing the mice population.

"What happened?" CeCe asked.

"I went over to the rival and distracted him with my feeble attempt at flirting. I wasn't expecting him to be so nice. And cute. He looked right at me like he was genuinely interested and smiled. He even kissed me on the cheek. Said to wait for him after the event." She touched her face and let out a shaky breath. "I should have told him about the practical joke. I wake up every morning regretting my actions."

"What was it? The joke?"

"Cutting a strap on the saddle of the bucking bronc he'd drawn for the event. Only, turned out, they cut four straps. Four important straps."

"Uh-oh."

"When the ten minutes were up, I hurried back to the boy, and he promptly blew me off. Said he wouldn't take me to a convenience store, much less the prom. His friends laughed and slapped him on the back. I was hurt and mad and embarrassed."

"The jerk. That's low."

"I ran off to the other side of the arena, looking for my sister. But I couldn't see anything. I was crying too hard. When I heard the announcer call the rival's name, I decided to watch him, thinking I could find a way to talk to him again after his ride. I pushed my way to the arena fence just as he and the bronc he was riding exploded from the chute." She paused, pain squeezing her insides at the memory.

"Hey, it's okay." Cece reached over and squeezed her hand. "You don't have tell me."

Kate swallowed a sob. Having started, she couldn't stop.

"After a few bucks, the saddle started to slip. The horse bucked again, and the saddle…" She faltered, feeling afresh the terror that had coursed through her. "He fell under the horse. Fourteen hundred pounds crashed down right on top of him."

"Oh, no!" CeCe gasped. "Did he…did he survive?"

"Yes."

"Thank the Lord."

"He was injured. Severely. The worst were fractures in his legs and his back and nerve damage to his spine. The doctors thought he'd spend the rest of his life a paraplegic."

"Kate. I'm sorry." CeCe put an arm around her.

"It was all my fault."

"It was those boys' fault. They cut the saddle straps."

"Which they couldn't have done without me."

"They would have found a way."

Kate sniffed and rubbed her nose. Many people, including Rosario, had told her the same thing. It made no difference. "Doesn't change the fact I helped them."

"You paid the price. Go easy on yourself."

She said nothing.

CeCe finished the last of her tea. "Whatever happened to him? The boy. Do you know?"

"He amazed his doctors and is walking."

She released a long gust of air. "That's incredible."

"He hasn't forgiven me."

"You can't know that."

"I do," Kate insisted, "and I don't blame him."

"Perhaps someday he'll come around."

"Perhaps." She gulped her tea, hoping to ease her parched throat. "It's Rand. He's the boy who got hurt. *Was* the boy."

"Rand!" CeCe's mouth fell open, and she sat back in her lawn chair. "Oh, wow. You're kidding."

"He's the reason I came here. To apologize and ask him for his forgiveness."

"Does Ansel know?"

"I told him everything before he hired me."

CeCe stared at Kate. "I'm going to need a little time to process this."

"I understand. And if you'd rather not be friends—"

"No, no. I like you. What happened—you were just a kid."

"Not that young. Eighteen."

"Young and taken advantage of," CeCe reiterated. "You've paid your debt to society. You regret what you did and changed your ways. I have no problem with you. In fact, I admire you. That Rand is…" She shook her head in astonishment. "He doesn't say much about the accident. Everybody knows he was bucked off during a rodeo, and that it's not a topic for discussion. But he's a good person, kind and fair. A first-rate manager."

"I'm glad he found a job and a home here at Still Water."

After a few minutes of quiet contemplation, CeCe stood and stretched her back. "I'm whipped and heading inside. You coming?"

"I'll be right along."

"Good night, Kate. See you in the morning."

Kate studied the cloudy sky until another movement from the stables caught her attention. She decided a short stroll to investigate might distract her enough she could get some sleep.

Soft nickers disrupted the silence as she walked the length of the aisle. Heads appeared over stall doors. She paused to pet a velvety nose here and scratch between a pair of stubby ears there. The familiar smells of hay and earth and horse acted like a salve, soothing old wounds.

"No cat that I can see," Kate told a curious sorrel gelding who sniffed her shirt with great interest and then bobbed his head as if disliking the lingering scent of laundry soap. "Guess I'll call it a night."

"What are you doing here?"

At the sound of Rand's voice, she whirled. Tension shot through her, though she attempted to present a composed front. "I was just clearing my head before going to bed."

"Not the stables. What are you doing at Still Water Ranch? And don't tell me it's because Ansel offered you a job. You could have refused him."

In the dark, beneath the dim yellow glow of the security lights, he appeared menacing. Older. Harder. Shadows brought out the sharp lines of his face as if drawn with the burnt end of a stick from the campfire. He was nothing like the sweet teenager who'd listened to Kate and kissed her cheek.

"I c-came to apologize. And ask f-for your forgiveness," she stammered.

"That's rich," he scoffed.

"Rand, please. I'm so s-sorry. Truly."

"I heard you talking to CeCe. You think you can win her and everyone else here over with your sob story."

Horror and shame filled her. "That's not why I told her."

"I don't like you, Kate. I don't trust you. And if it were up to me, you'd be gone by morning." He leveled a finger at her. "But since it's not up to me, and we have no choice except to work together, I'm warning you to stay out of my way."

In all the scenarios she'd imagined, none of them had Rand spewing such loathing and anger at her. She felt the chill from his icy glare pierce her damaged heart. Without another word, he stormed off, leaving her alone with her shock and despair.

Kate crept back to the bunkhouse, willing away the tears that threatened to fall. If not for having promised Ansel she'd stay a full week, she'd pack up her few belongings and leave right then and there. But Kate was the kind of person who, when she gave her word, kept it.

As she climbed the bunkhouse steps, she spotted a pale, narrow face with stringy dark hair staring out at her from the window. One of the youth camp members? Had she been watching Kate and listening to her and Rand?

The next second, the face disappeared, almost as if it had never been there. By the time Kate entered the bunkhouse, all was quiet except for someone in the corner bed snoring softly.

Crawling into her bed, she buried herself beneath the covers. Hard as she tried, she couldn't shake off her sense of foreboding.

Chapter Three

Kate dropped her bulky backpack onto her freshly made bed and unzipped the main compartment. Per Rand's instructions, she could bring personal items weighing no more than five pounds.

All around her, the youth camp members busied themselves getting ready for the trail ride. Arguments ensued about who was next in line for the bathroom. Sleeping bags were rolled up and crammed into their sacks for taking along. Missing boots were hunted down. One girl screamed because she thought the hair tie beneath her cot was a spider.

"Welcome to youth camp," a middle-aged woman said with a laugh.

"It's not so bad. I've stayed in communal housing before." Truthfully, the commotion reminded her a little of prison.

"I'm Margie, by the way." The woman extended her hand, which Kate shook.

"You a wrangler here?"

She laughed, and the spare tire at her waist jiggled.

Elaborate tattoos climbed the length of both forearms. "Do I look like a wrangler to you?"

"Well…" Kate lifted a shoulder. "You could be."

"I'm in charge of the mama and baby horses. The mamas are in my care from the moment they step onto the ranch, and the babies from the moment they're born." She beamed broadly. "They're all my sweetums. Every one of them."

"It's nice to meet you."

Margie glanced at Kate's open backpack. "That's quite a collection you have there."

"I like to keep everything in one place. Easily accessible that way."

"I once knew a homeless fellow who carried all his belongings with him."

"Oh?" Being homeless was when and how Kate had started the practice of keeping her possessions with her. Transitioning after her release from prison hadn't been easy, and she'd spent a few months without a roof over her head.

"Is that pepper spray?" Margie asked, peering into the backpack.

"It is." Assured that all her things were intact, and nothing had disappeared during the night, Kate began removing the items she planned to take on the trail ride. Her phone. A charging cable and portable battery. Her IDs, bank debit card and cash secured in a small wallet. A couple of power bars. The can of pepper spray and a pocketknife. She transferred the items into a fanny pack, which she fastened around her waist.

"Expecting trouble on the ride?" Margie asked.

"You can never be too careful." Another lesson Kate had learned during her homeless days. Protect herself from attack and protect her possessions from being stolen. Replacements were often hard to come by.

The other woman raised her brows. "I suppose not."

Kate took the opportunity to exit their conversation. She returned the backpack to the metal chest at the foot of her bed. Before closing the lid and engaging the lock, she removed a clean shirt, a clean pair of socks and a light jacket. She then stuffed the shirt and socks in the sleeves of the jacket.

A few minutes later, she emerged from the chaos of the bunkhouse and into the overcast morning. The clouds lay heavy in the sky. It would rain today. The questions were, when and how hard?

Adjusting her frayed cowboy hat, she tucked the jacket beneath her arm. Before heading to the office, she made a quick stop at her truck for her own sleeping bag. With each step, she attempted to banish Rand from her thoughts, yet her glance flitted from one spot to the next as if searching him out. He'd show eventually. He was leading the trail ride.

Kate had considered leaving Still Water Ranch at the crack of dawn but changed her mind. She refused to let Rand chase her off. More importantly, she'd promised Ansel she'd stay a week, and Kate kept her word.

The cook's SUV was parked in front of the office, its rear door opened. A crowd had gathered as burritos were distributed. The ranch dogs made pests of themselves, begging treats. Kate fetched a cup of lukewarm coffee, downed it in several long swallows, and then got in line.

"Morning," the cook said when Kate's turn came. "One or two?" The plain but kindly faced older woman handed Kate a warm, foil wrapped burrito.

"One's plenty."

"You sure? They're small, and lunch is a long way off. You're going to work up an appetite today."

"Um…"

"Give her another one."

A jolt went through her at the familiar deep voice. She didn't need to look behind her to know that Rand stood there. The hairs rising on the back of her neck told her.

"Do you take this much interest in what the other wranglers eat?" she asked.

"As a matter of fact, I do. Your welfare on this ride is my responsibility."

Before she could object, Mrs. Sciacca pressed a second burrito into Kate's free hand. "Condiments and napkins are over there." She indicated a small portable table set up near the SUV. "You'll find the box lunches in the crate beside them. Hope you like peanut butter and jelly sandwiches."

"Thank you."

Kate hurried to the condiment table, where she unwrapped her burritos. Savoring the smell of eggs, cheese and chorizo, she added hot sauce and jalapeños. Finding a post by the office to lean against, she set down her load and devoured the first burrito.

She really needed to eat slower. People were staring. People like Rand, who stood at the hood of the SUV. He and the other wranglers were using the hood like a table, eating as they examined a map.

Why had he insisted she take two burritos? It wasn't as if he cared about her or her *welfare*. He'd probably be happy if she missed breakfast altogether.

No, that was unkind. And he was depending on her

help with the trail ride. She'd be no good to anyone if she became lightheaded from hunger.

After finishing her meal, she disposed of her trash and then grabbed one of the last remaining box lunches. It would go in her saddlebags, along with her extra clothes. By then, most everyone had left. Only Mrs. Sciacca and a few of the helpers like CeCe and Margie remained. The last of the youth camp members were heading toward the corral. Kate rushed after them.

The other wranglers were already there, including Rand. Several horses stood tied to the corral fence, ready to be groomed and saddled. More were being haltered and led from the corral.

Rand came over her, a slight limp to his gait. Was the weather bothering his legs?

"You're late."

"I'm sorry." There she went, apologizing again.

"Here's a list of which horse is assigned to which camper." He produced a piece of paper and held it out to her. "Have the kids start grooming and saddling."

"How do I know which horse is which?"

He blew out a breath. For a moment, she thought he was going to snatch the paper out of her hand and assign the task to someone else.

"The horses' names are on their halters," he said with a note of impatience.

"And where's the grooming equipment?"

This time, he drew in a breath. A long one.

She squared her shoulders in response. "I can't be expected to know where everything is without being told first."

A stern emotion crossed his face. Subtle, but there, and then it vanished. She thought she might have surprised him by standing up for herself. That, or she'd made him angry again.

"In the back of the pickup." He hitched his chin at an old Ford parked nearby, its tailgate lowered. "The kids know which saddles and bridles are theirs and can carry them from the tack building."

"Gotcha."

At the corral fence, she checked the name on the halter of the nearest horse tied to the fence, and then located the corresponding youth camp member's name on her list.

"Is Serene here?" She scrutinized the dozen kids, some helping, others talking or goofing off. "Serene? Where are you?"

"What?" came an annoyed response from the other side of the truck.

"Front and center." After a moment when the girl didn't show, Kate said with less patience, "Come on, Serene, get a move on."

At last, a tall, willowy girl with stringy black hair materialized and eyed Kate warily. She recognized the girl as the one she'd seen in the bunkhouse window last night. Rather than ask about it, she kept her mouth shut. Kate wasn't worried or afraid—prison had toughened her—as much as curious. Instead, she'd wait for Serene to acknowledge her, if she did.

A shorter girl with raggedy brown hair that might have been cut with a pair of child's scissors followed behind Serene. Kate had noticed the two of them in the bunkhouse and concluded they were inseparable.

"Hey, Serene. You're on Flapjack here." Kate patted the knobby-kneed bay beside her displaying the gentle demeanor of a trail ride veteran.

"I've been riding that horse." She pointed to a gray still in the corral.

"Well, this is the horse you're assigned to today."

"I don't want him." Serene crossed her arms over her concave waist.

"I'll ride him," her friend offered.

"What's your name?" Kate asked.

"Brie. Like the cheese."

"That's a nice name."

The girl smiled.

"You're on…" Kate studied the string of horses. "Little Red."

"Cool."

Serene gave Brie a small shove. "That horse is fat and lazy. You want another one."

"Oh…okay." Brie flinched and peered up at Kate, uncertainty on her face. "Can, um, I have a different horse?"

"How about you give Little Red a try," Kate suggested. "Then, if she's not a good fit for you, we'll see if you can swap with someone else at lunch."

Brie nodded, only to worry her lower lip when her friend glared at her. "She said I can swap at lunch."

"Whatever." Serene rolled her eyes and huffed in irritation.

Kate brought Little Red over, deciding she'd pay extra attention to this pair of youth camp members. Brie, especially. Kate saw a bit of herself in the shorter girl, having lived in the shadow of an older sibling with a bigger, more forceful personality. If Kate had learned to stand up to her sister, developed confidence, she might not have ended up duped by a cute boy and paid a dear price.

She tied the compact mare next to Flapjack and got the two girls started on grooming and cleaning hooves.

Having been at the ranch a few days already, they knew that much. Satisfied they were doing an adequate job, she found two more camp members and paired them with their horses. Then two more.

Before long, all dozen kids were readying their mounts. The weather was the main topic of conversation.

"We'll make it to camp before the rain hits," Rand said with assurance. "If it even does hit. The wind could drive the clouds away."

Kate was unconvinced.

By the time she returned to Serene and Brie, they'd saddled and bridled their two mounts. Kate inspected their handiwork. She tightened the girth on Serene's horse and shortened the stirrups on Brie's. Meanwhile, one of the other wranglers loaded tents, a cookstove, folding shovels and other camping equipment on their two packhorses.

"Good job," Kate told the girls. "Don't forget to grab a canteen. Everyone's responsible for their own water."

"You have a phone?" Serene asked.

"Yes. Why?"

"Can I borrow it? I need to make a call."

Ansel had warned Kate about this very thing. Camp members had to give up their phones during their stay. It was part of the agreement. For some, this was the hardest rule to follow, and they'd cajole and bargain with the ranch staff and occasionally lie in an attempt to get their hands on a phone.

"Sorry. You'll have to ask Mr. Laurent if you can use the ranch phone."

"But it's an emergency," the girl whined.

"All the more reason to talk to him."

"Fine." She exaggerated the *F* and stomped off, dragging Brie along with her.

Kate watched them go, murmuring to herself, "God never gives us more than we can handle."

"What was that all about?"

Naturally, Rand had sauntered over.

"One of the girls wanted to use my phone."

"You told her no." A statement rather than a question.

"Yes, Rand. I told her no."

"Good. Now get your horse and saddle up. We leave in thirty minutes."

"Will do."

"Your job is to bring up the rear."

Ansel arrived then, and the pace accelerated. Between checking on the kids and readying her own horse, Kate was in constant motion. That didn't stop her from noticing Rand's frequent glances aimed at her.

What was with him, anyway? For someone who'd insisted she stay out of his way, he constantly sought her out.

Mega Max's horseshoes clanged against the sharp rocks as he climbed the steep mountainside. Sides heaving, his nose close to the ground, he put all his weight into his shoulders. Rand was glad to have such a strong, surefooted horse to ride. That way, he could let Mega Max do the work while he concentrated his attention on the kids, other wranglers and packhorses forming a long line behind him. Their safety was his number-one priority.

That included Kate. He may not want her here, but he'd see to it nothing bad happened to her while she was in his charge.

He glanced backward, making sure none of the kids or their mounts were having problems. This half-mile stretch of winding and rugged trail wasn't for the faint of heart and was the worst they'd encounter on their ride.

Everyone appeared to be holding their own. Some chatted nervously. Others concentrated on the uneven ground. A few panicked and clung to their saddle horns, which was to be expected. What about Kate? She was too far back for Rand to see her expression. But she rode with confidence, her posture indicating she wasn't scared of her horse slipping and tumbling over the side.

Had she ever ridden the Superstition Mountains before, or gone on any trail ride for that matter? Her job application revealed little other than listing the various jobs she'd had since her release, her education and some personal references. Not much else. Not even her stint courtesy of the state.

Yes, he'd read her employment file, though he wasn't sure what he'd expected to find there. Something else to blame on her? Not a reason to forgive her. That couldn't be found on a piece of paper.

Nor would it ever be found, not when he remained closed and refused to consider such a thing. His previous conversation with Ansel returned. Letting bygones be bygones felt like too much. Rand wasn't ready. Not yet. Could he be at some point? That he'd even consider forgiving Kate took him aback. He'd always resisted. Then again, he hadn't seen the ravages of what she'd been through, so clear in her appearance and manner. Kate had suffered, and Rand wasn't made of stone.

At the top of the incline, the land flattened out. He reined to a stop and waited until all sixteen of them had gathered in a wide spot. They'd passed two groups of hikers along the way. In the far distance, across the wide ravine, a line of six or seven riders moved slowly along a different trail. People were out, just not in the same numbers as on a sunny day.

"We'll take a five-minute break to give the horses a rest," Rand announced. "Don't forget to drink water." He unwound the strap of his canteen hanging from his saddle horn and unscrewed the lid. "You need to stay hydrated."

A faint boom sounded as he finished drinking. Rand studied the distant mountaintop, listening hard, but heard only the kids chattering and the screech of a hawk flying overhead. No lightning in the overcast sky, so the boom hadn't been thunder. What then?

"Hey, everyone," he called out and pointed skyward. "See that? It's a red-tailed hawk."

"Awesome," said one of the boys.

"Is that real?" Aiesha asked.

Rand chuckled. "Out here, what else would it be?"

"A drone?"

"It's a hawk. Trust me."

At that moment, a light drizzle began to fall. There went Rand's prediction that the rain would hold off until they reached their campsite.

"It's pouring," Serene wailed as if she'd melt.

"It's sprinkling," Rand countered and then louder to the group, "Get your ponchos out of your saddlebags."

That triggered a flurry of activity. He noticed Kate had dismounted, tied her horse to the knotty shrub branch and was going from one kid to the next, helping them with their ponchos. She'd done that without being asked.

Rand also dismounted and donned his poncho. He then walked a few feet over to a high point, fished his phone from his pocket and called the ranch office. After a minute of silence, he hung up and dialed again. This time, the call went through.

Grandpa Billy answered with a gravelly, "Hello. Still Water Ranch."

"It's Rand."

"Hey, buddy. How goes the ride?"

Static made it hard to understand the older man. "Fine other than a little rain. What about you?"

"Dry as a bone here."

Rand glanced again at the sky. Arizona's monsoons were nothing if not unpredictable. Rain often fell in the mountains and nowhere else. "Well, hopefully it's a passing shower."

His remark was met by empty air.

"Grandpa Billy? You there?"

The connection went dead, and Rand repocketed his phone. Reception was hit or miss in the Superstitions on a clear day. Poor to nonexistent during inclement weather.

Sensing he was being watched, he glanced around the group and then at the mountains toward where he'd sworn he heard a boom. When he turned back around, he found Serene had moved closer.

"What is it?" he asked.

Her stare didn't waver. "Nothing."

His skin itched in a way he didn't like. He'd seen that expression before on other youth camp members who were plotting no good.

"Break's over," he abruptly said. "Let get going."

As he mounted, a second faint boom sounded. "Anybody hear that?"

"Hear what, Rand?" Murry asked.

He and Scotty were leading the packhorses. Reliable and levelheaded, they'd been Rand's first picks for wranglers on the ride. His other first pick had been replaced by Kate.

"A boom," Rand said, hitching his chin. "In that direction."

"Not me."

"Probably thunder."

Rand's nerves were fraying. The rain must be getting to him. And so was Kate. And the way the girl Serene had stared at him.

Once the ride resumed, he relaxed. No more distant booms. The boy riding behind him, Cayden, asked endless questions, which served to distract Rand.

"Grandpa Billy was talking about a mountain lion. Are they for real?"

"They are," Rand said.

"We gonna see one?"

"I'd be very surprised. They're solitary animals and more afraid of us than we are of them."

"My brother showed me a video online where a mountain lion chased this dude."

"That's rare."

"Grandpa Billy also said to be on the lookout for a gold mine. If I find it, I could be rich." Cayden whooped with excitement.

"The Lost Dutchman's Mine."

"Yeah, that's what he called it."

"Sorry to be the bearer of bad news, pal." Rand shifted and flexed his calves. His legs, always a little sore, had started to ache after hours in the saddle. "Thousands of people have searched for the Lost Dutchman's Mine since the late nineteen hundreds. No one's found it yet. I wouldn't count on you being the one."

"Aw, bummer."

An hour later, they reached the spot along the trail where Rand had planned to stop for lunch. The timing couldn't be better. The kids were getting hungry and restless, and the rain had increased from a drizzle to a steady light downfall. Rand decided to skip visiting the ruins left by the mountains' first Indigenous inhabitants and continue straight to camp. That way, they could set up their tents before the rain fell in earnest.

"What's that?" Cayden asked. "I thought you said no motorized vehicles were allowed up here."

Rand frowned. The far-off whine could only be an engine. "I don't know. Maybe the forest service is up here cutting trees. Or some campers."

Which made no sense, given the rain. Unless someone was in trouble. He hoped not.

"Tie your horse to the nearest branch," he instructed to the group. "And stay close. No wandering off alone under any circumstances. If you need to head off to the bushes for some privacy, take someone with you."

"Then it wouldn't be private," Serene quipped.

Rand chose not to respond.

As the kids removed their box lunches and plastic bottles of fruit punch, they split off into pairs and trios and found places to sit. Serene got into a squabble with another girl about sharing the toilet paper. Rand considered intervening, but Kate beat him to it and, he had to admit, quickly diffused the situation.

Finding a boulder, Rand sat and devoured his sandwich, apple, hard-boiled egg and cookie. From the corner of his eye, he watched Kate, who conversed with

Murry. They shared a fallen log. She listened more than talked as Murry regaled her with stories of life at Still Water Ranch.

Rand told himself he didn't care if his coworker wanted to pursue her. When convincing himself of that became harder and harder, he stood, stuffed his trash in his saddlebag and made a round of the horses. A few girths required tightening, and a few saddles had slipped out of place after the long trek up the mountain. Hearing Serene's whiny voice, he turned.

"I'm gonna puke."

"Are you feeling sick?" Kate asked with concern.

"Sick of that lunch. It was gross." She made a fake retching sound.

"You ate all of it."

"I was starving."

"So, you're not sick, then."

Serene rolled her eyes. "I want a different horse."

Kate surveyed the group. "Anyone here willing to trade horses with Serene?"

"Nope."

"No way."

"Not me."

"Sorry, Serene," Kate said. "You're stuck with Flapjack."

She groaned as if in agony.

"He's a good horse and has done a worthy job carrying you on this hard trail. You should appreciate him rather than want to be rid of him."

"He's ugly."

"Looks aren't everything."

Rand watched the two of them with interest. Kate

dealt with the preteen firmly, yet patiently. Where did she learn that?

Suddenly, Serene whirled and jabbed Brie in the chest with her index finger. "You trade horses with me."

Brie retreated a step. "I… I…like Little Red."

"I said, trade with me. Now."

"I…"

Kate pushed off the log. "Stop bullying her."

"What?" Anger flashed in Serene's eyes. "I'm not bullying her."

"You are. And you're going to stop right now, or the both of us are heading straight back to the ranch, and Mr. Laurent will send for your foster parents."

Serene faltered only to regain her composure and square her shoulders. "You can't do that."

"I can and I will. The ride will continue without us."

The battle waging inside the girl played out on her face. She wanted to stay. She also didn't want to concede.

Kate walked over to Serene and placed a hand on her shoulder. Every pair of eyes there watched intently.

"We all have choices," Kate said, kinder than before. "You can make the right one, or the wrong one. And bullying Brie is the wrong one."

Rand couldn't agree more. He'd been bullied, by his rival and buddies who'd sabotaged his saddle. If Kate hadn't stepped in to handle the escalating situation with the two foster sisters, he would have in a heartbeat.

"What do you know?" The girl shrugged off Kate's hand.

"I know I've made more than my share of wrong choices," she said. "One really wrong choice landed me in prison for six years."

A few soft gasps and one "Seriously, dude," erupted from the group. Brie stared at Kate, awestruck. Murry had the opposite reaction and scooted to the edge of the log as if putting more distance between him and where Kate had sat.

"Bullying isn't a crime," Serene mumbled.

"Actually," Kate said, "it is. When it's extreme and leads to a tragic outcome, it's very much a crime. You don't want to end up like me. Living your life regretting your actions."

Rand expected her to meet his gaze and waited. Only she didn't. She remained focused on Serene.

"Okay, okay," Serene quipped. "I won't trade horses. I'll ride stupid Flapjack."

"Good." Kate nodded. "Because I don't want to miss camping out in this rain."

Her stab at humor and her smile relaxed the group. For the most part, Serene and Murry both avoided her. For some reason Rand couldn't explain, that bothered him. Murry, especially.

Though it was nearing time to resume the ride, Rand strolled over to where Kate stood next to her horse, refastening her saddlebag. She looked up at his approach but didn't turn to face him.

"Hey," he said.

"Hi."

She zipped up her fanny pack but not before he saw a white can with lettering across the front.

"Is that pepper spray?"

"Yes."

"There aren't any bears up here."

She sighed. "What do you want, Rand?"

He had come on a little strong and dialed it down a

few notches. "Just to say, you handled the situation with Serene well."

"Thanks."

"You work with kids before?"

"No. I guess some of the prison counseling sessions have rubbed off on me."

He gave her a frank once-over. "I wasn't expecting you to admit your stint in prison to the kids."

"I'm not ashamed of my past, Rand, and I'm not going to hide from it. If I can use my experiences to help others, then I will. And if people like you and Murry don't want anything to do with me, that's your loss."

Two days ago, he wouldn't have argued with her. Suddenly, he was less sure. As he walked back to his horse, he felt a crack form in his once impenetrable armor.

Chapter Four

Before mounting up, Rand tried to reach the ranch again. The rain had slowed and then stopped altogether during lunch, much to his relief. The skies, however, remained ominous. Dense gray clouds promised rainfall later in the day. The return ride tomorrow morning would be a wet one.

Hitting Speed Dial, he waited…and waited. After a full minute of silence, he disconnected. He set his phone on the boulder beside him and rubbed a kink in the back of his neck.

Before he could ask Scotty to try his phone, the faint hum of an engine distracted him. It had to be a chain saw. But who would be cutting trees in this weather?

"Scotty!" he hollered, "did you h—"

"Mr. Rand, Mr. Rand. Help me!"

He stood. "What's wrong, Aiesha?"

"My horse is bleeding."

Rand made his way over. "Where?"

"There. Look."

He bent to examine the injury. Her horse indeed had a gash on his front leg, a few inches above the hoof. Minor, thank goodness, and the bleeding had long stopped. The horse had probably cut his leg on a jagged rock or protruding branch.

"He'll be fine," he told Aiesha and straightened.

"What am I gonna do if I can't ride?" Tears filled her eyes.

"You can ride him. Horses are pretty tough animals."

"Really?"

"Really. It's no worse than you getting a cut on your arm. Let me grab some ointment from my saddlebag. After we make camp, I want you to wash his leg with water and apply more ointment."

As he retrieved the tube of medicine, he noticed Kate giving the other kids a leg up onto their horses and checking their tack. She caught him watching her and stiffened. Rand nodded, but she didn't respond. When he finished tending Aiesha's horse, he helped her on and then returned to the boulder for his phone.

Only it wasn't there. He automatically patted his jeans pockets and checked his saddlebags. No phone, not that he'd expected to find it. He knew with certainty he'd left the phone on the boulder.

"Murry." He motioned to the wrangler. "Do me a favor and call my phone, would you? I can't find it."

Murry did. Rand listened and heard only silence.

"Has anyone seen my phone?" His gaze took in the line of riders and horses. "I put it right here."

His question was met with head shakes, shrugs and a chorus of noes. His gaze found Serene.

She squared her slim shoulders and raised her chin. "Why you staring at me?"

"Have you seen my phone, Serene?"

"No, I ain't seen it."

"Brie?" Kate asked. "What about you?"

She was smart to question Serene's partner in crime. Brie wasn't as tough as her foster sister.

"No, Ms. Kate," the girl insisted. "I swear I haven't seen it."

Rand believed her. He couldn't say the same about Serene and was convinced a search of her belongings would reveal his phone. She was smart and had probably silenced the ringer.

What, he debated, should he do? Confront the girl and cause a scene or wait until he could deal with her privately? He chose the latter. She didn't know his pass code, and neither would she get any reception in this weather. His biggest worry was that she'd toss the phone down a ravine when she realized it was useless to her.

Resigned, he swung into the saddle. *Please let nothing else go wrong today.*

"All right, everyone. Let's move out. We have about three hours to reach camp. Longer if we make a lot of stops."

He watched as Kate resumed her position at the end of the line. Tomorrow, he decided, he'd let her switch with Murry and lead one of the packhorses if she wanted.

As Rand was about to nudge Max into a walk, he noticed a pair of hikers appearing from around the bend behind Kate. They were dressed in rugged outerwear from head to toe, including their rain gear, and carried bulging backpacks with sleeping bags fastened to the top. Serious outdoor enthusiasts, for sure. Those backpacks weighed forty pounds at least.

As they neared, the taller hiker waved in greeting. "Hello."

Murry waved back. "Howdy."

The pair stepped off the trail and went wide, circumventing the line of horses and riders. Rand appreciated the precaution. Other hikers on previous trail rides had walked right into the horses, causing problems.

"You heading to the ruins, too?" the taller one asked Rand when he approached.

Only then did Rand realize the man's companion was a woman. She appeared equally fit and strong, managing her heavy load with ease.

"Thought about it," Rand answered. "But with the possibility of rain, we're heading straight to our campsite."

"Where's that?"

He was hesitant to answer, which was probably silly. Anyone wanting to find them could. Kids were a rowdy bunch, and noise carried in the mountains. He thought again of the engine and booms he wasn't fully convinced were thunder. But one could never be too careful with strangers.

"The meadow by the springs," he finally said. "There's plenty of grass and water for the horses."

The man smiled with approval. "Nice spot. We're staying near Reavis Ranch."

"That's a long hike for one day. You sure you can make it?"

The man exchanged glances with the woman.

She nodded. "We're sure."

"If we don't," the man said, "we'll just pick out a good spot and camp. We've got everything we need."

"Choose a high place where the water won't collect," Rand advised. "Just in case the rain worsens."

The man squinted at the sky. "There's a chance this

will blow over by nightfall." He lowered his head, his expression dubious. "And a chance it won't."

"Which is a good reason for us to get a move on," Rand told the hikers. "We'll give you a head start."

"You stay safe." The man took a step, only to hesitate. "Did you hear a sound earlier, like an engine?"

"Yeah."

"I thought motorized vehicles weren't allowed in the Superstitions."

"They aren't. Could be a chain saw."

"Strange." The man shrugged before he and his companion continued up the trail.

Rand waited until the hikers were well ahead, despite protests from the restless kids. A strong breeze swept over him from the east and with it, the scent of rain. They had best get to camp pronto.

"Walk out, boy." He nudged Mega Max in the flanks. With a lusty snort, the gelding started forward.

Rand's nerves gradually settled. He knew these mountains like the back of his hand and had ridden this particular trail fifty times. The kids' horses were sturdy and reliable. He had no doubt they would all be fine. Soggy and dirty when they got back to the ranch, and in need of a hot shower, but also having had an experience they'd never forget.

He called to Murry behind him. "When we reach the summit ahead, try calling the ranch."

"Will do."

Thirty minutes later, they crested the rise. A spectacular view of the valley lay before them. The sight of God's handiwork never failed to fill Rand with awe. Today, the rain had painted a vivid green sheen over the landscape, reminding him of an antique painting on display in Ansel's living room.

Rand wasn't fooled, however. Danger lurked in these mountains. Rattlesnakes and Gila monsters. Poisonous insects. Javelina and the rare mountain lion. The sodden ground was deceiving and could collapse without warning. Rockslides weren't uncommon and flash floods a regular occurrence.

He knew enough to be careful and keep everyone safe. Murry and Scotty were equally experienced. They'd have no problem as long as they stayed on the trail.

"Everyone, look over there." He pointed, determined to keep the mood light. "See that big column rising up? It's called Weaver's Needle, named after the mountain man Pauline Weaver."

Aiesha laughed. "Isn't Pauline a girl's name?"

"Didn't used to be."

Cayden stood up in his stirrups, his eyes bright. "Grandpa Billy said that's where the Lost Dutchman's Mine is. He says the shadow points to the mine's location. Can we go?"

"Sorry, buddy," Rand said. "For one, it's too far. More than a day's ride from here. For another, thousands of people have searched the area and nobody's found the mine."

"Ah, man." Cayden plopped back down in the saddle, dejected.

"Scotty, did you reach the ranch?"

"Still no service," the older man answered.

Kate tried, too, also without success.

They resumed their ride, the trail growing increasingly steeper and more difficult. To their right, close enough to reach out and touch, the mountainside rose, a giant wall five stories high. Prickly pear and cholla cacti jutted out from the wall. Sage and creosote bushes lined the trail. Colorful blossoms dotted the scraggly flora, inviting bees and birds. At the bottom of the ravine, an army of saguaro cacti stood at attention, their arms raised.

"They're saying hello." Cayden laughed at his own joke.

Two and a half hours, and two short breaks later, they arrived at the springs where they'd camp for the night. And the good news was, ahead of the rain. It broke just as they were unpacking the tents.

"Murry," Rand said as he tossed a nylon bag holding one of the four-man tents they'd brought onto the ground. "You and Kate oversee the kids and horses. Scotty and I will set up the tents and the canopies. Kids, unsaddle your horses and help unload the packhorses. All the cooking gear goes under the blue canopy. Saddles and tack, under the green one."

"My sleeping bag is getting wet," Serene complained.

"The sack is waterproof. Just don't remove the sleeping bag until you're inside your tent."

"You sure?" The girl stood beside her horse, hugging her thin frame through her poncho.

"I'm sure." He'd guess she was more anxious than cold. "Now, unsaddle Flapjack."

With a grumble, she lifted the stirrup and reached for the girth buckle.

As the rain increased, Serene wasn't the only one complaining. Cayden alone remained impervious to the downpour. Perpetually cheerful and with a natural curiosity about everything, he talked nonstop.

"Grandpa Billy says if you want the rainbow, you have to put up with the rain."

Apparently, he and Grandpa Billy were hanging out a lot. Rand had to smile. It was probably good for both of them. God had a way of putting the right people together.

Rand watched Kate across the meadow, tying horses beneath trees for cover and divvying up the pellets they'd brought along. The horses would also eat the grass at their feet down to the nubs by morning, rain or no rain.

Did God have a reason for bringing her back into Rand's life? He had sometimes questioned the Almighty's purpose, but he also trusted Him implicitly. Whatever the outcome, it would be for the best.

"How we gonna cook in the rain?" Serene asked on a long whine.

"How do you think?" Cayden quipped. "Just like the prospectors did in the old days."

Serene groaned and rolled her eyes.

"The prospectors didn't have a nylon canopy," Rand said with amusement. "Or a kerosene cookstove. Who's hungry for chili dogs?"

"Me, me!"

"First we need to finish setting up camp."

Before long, the tents were readied, the horses settled, kerosene lanterns lit and hanging from hooks beneath the canopies, flashlights distributed and dinner, such as it was, dished onto paper plates.

"Any volunteer to say grace?" Rand asked.

None of the kids answered. No surprise there. He was about to start when Kate raised a hand.

"I will."

Not the person he expected. "All right."

Standing beside the canopy, she bowed her head. Others did the same. When she spoke, her voice rang out clear and with conviction.

"Lord, thank You for this day. For guiding us safely to camp and for showing us the splendor of Your many wonders along the way. Please watch over us tonight while we sleep. Thank You for this food and for our friends here with us and, most of all, for Your many blessings. Amen."

A chorus of amens followed, including Rand's.

He liked the simplicity of her prayer and the heartfelt emotion that came through. She was a person truly grateful for this day.

Despite the increasing rain, supper was a jovial event. Along with the chili dogs, they had individual serving cups of applesauce and pudding for dessert. Packaged food traveled better on the rough trail and tended not to break open. Scotty regaled the group with stories of Elisha Reavis. The eccentric recluse had built a ranch house, planted an apple orchard that still produced fruit today and found a way to grow produce in the middle of the Superstitions not far from where they were camping. Each year, he transported his harvest to town and sold it to the locals. With each visit, the stories about him and his escapades grew.

Everyone helped with postdinner cleanup, then the kids started for the tents or remained beneath the canopy, talking. While Rand bent over the small ice chest they'd brought along, reorganizing the contents, a sharp report split the night air. He instantly straightened, his heart pounding and all his senses on high alert.

Not a boom and not thunder. There was no mistaking the sound of a gunshot.

* * *

"Get down!" Kate whirled, her instincts urging her to run. She'd witnessed more than her share of violence in prison and while living on the streets and knew enough to hide.

Except this wasn't prison or the streets.

"Was that a gunshot?" Brie asked. Her poncho hood had fallen low over her forehead but failed to hide her anxious expression.

She wasn't alone. Kate noticed several other kids had covered their heads with their arms and ducked. Many resided in the poorer sections of Phoenix and, like Kate, were sadly familiar with the sounds of gunfire. Those inside the tents emerged, some cautiously, others hastily.

"Everyone, over there!" She waved her arm toward the stand of mesquite trees. Out in the open like this, they were easy targets. "Hurry!"

The kids scrambled toward the trees, some more quickly than others.

Kate went with them, insisting they sit on the ground beneath the shelter of the trees.

Where was Rand? She'd seen him earlier, and now he was gone. Scotty and Murry were with the startled horses, making sure none of them got loose, but Rand was nowhere in sight.

Dear Lord. Please, please, please. Let him be okay.

"The branches are scratchy." Serene pushed at an offending limb.

Kate fought to remain calm. Rand, wherever he was, would want her to insure all the kids remained safe and, for the moment, they were. "Stay here until we know what's going on. Don't come out until me or one of the other wranglers gives you the all clear."

"Where are you going, Ms. Kate?" Brie asked in a thready voice.

Only then did Kate realize she was on the move. "I'll be right back." She had to find Rand.

Before she got twenty feet, a hand emerged from the darkness and clamped on to her arm with a force that meant business. It might as well have been squeezing her lungs, for her breath escaped in a single harsh gust.

"Kate."

She twisted and stared up into Rand's determined brown eyes. Just like that, her lungs began to function again, and her fear fled.

"Rand! You're all right."

"Are you? You seem shaken."

She shoved the memories of prison and the streets from her mind, concentrating instead on his touch. She couldn't remember the last time someone made her feel safe and secure with a single, simple gesture. Rand was the last person in the world she'd expect to evoke those sensations in her.

"Tell me that wasn't a gunshot."

He pulled her farther into the shadows and out of view. "Handgun, I think. Not a rifle."

"You can tell?"

"Different firearms make distinct sounds."

Wow. Impressive and scary.

Murry and Scotty stood nearby, their gazes continually traveling in the direction the gunfire had come from. Scotty cracked a nervous joke. His and Murry's laughs came off strained.

"Why is someone shooting up here?" Kate asked. "That makes no sense."

Rand relaxed his grip on her but didn't let go. "Could

be target practice. Could be someone shooting at a mountain lion or a snake."

"Or someone being stupid."

"That, too," he conceded.

"Don't they realize other people are nearby?"

"It came from that direction." Rand hitched his chin toward the top of the hill several hundred yards away. "We're not that close."

"Close enough for a bullet to reach."

"Let's not jump to conclusions. There hasn't been another shot."

She could see he was trying to believe his own words.

"Maybe we should go home."

Rand peered at the sky. Water that had pooled in the brim of his cowboy hat poured down his back.

On any normal early evening in June, the sun would still be shining. Tonight, heavy clouds cast them in near darkness. The rain had increased into a full-fledged storm since they'd reached camp. Lightning flashed in the east, illuminating the entire sky with a network of jagged bolts. Thunder boomed like cannon shots.

"We can't go home," he said. "Not in the dark. Not in this weather. It's too dangerous. We could get lost. The rocks are slick, and the ground could give way. Someone might fall or get struck by lightning. It's rare but not unheard of."

She knew he was right. Still, her gut screamed at her that danger loomed. And she'd been on her own too much these last four years not to follow her instincts. "The horses are surefooted and trustworthy."

"Kate, I know you're worried. I am, too. But we're better off remaining in the tents and leaving first thing in the morning."

"What if there's still thunder and lightning?"

Murry and Scotty chose that moment to wander over, hunching their shoulders and keeping their heads low.

"What do you think?" Scotty asked, eyeing Rand's hand on Kate's arm.

Rand instantly released her. "Let's move all the tents beneath the trees. Without alarming the kids," he added. "Lay the extra tarps on the tent floors. Be sure their sleeping bags are on top of the foam pads and have no contact with the ground." He turned to Murry. "Were you able to reach the ranch?"

"Nope." The other wrangler gave his head a dismal shake.

Kate had tried her own phone right before the gunshot, also without success.

"All we can do, then, is settle in for the night," Rand said.

"Won't be the first time I've slept outside in a thunderstorm," Scotty mused.

They all were acting much too casual as far as Kate was concerned. "What about the gunshot? We can't just ignore it."

"No, we can't." Rand wiped away water that had dripped down his neck.

"I heard two explosions on the way up here," she said. "In the same direction as the gunshot."

Murry dismissed her with a chortle. "That was thunder."

"No, it wasn't."

Rand had a different reaction. "Why didn't you say something?" he demanded.

How to explain that Murry wasn't the first person to dismiss Kate's concerns? Granted, she did sometimes overreact. She couldn't help herself. It was a leftover from prison life and postprison life. PTSD. A heightened sense of survival. Whatever one called it, the result was the same. Kate feared the worst and let her imagination run wild.

"I was waiting for the right moment," she answered softly.

Murry turned to face Rand. "This is ridiculous. We're letting a little thunderstorm mess with our heads."

"Not just a thunderstorm," Rand reiterated. "A gunshot and multiple explosions."

Kate glanced over at the kids, who watched the adults with interest.

"I think we should take turns standing guard," she told Rand. "You said yourself we can't take any chances with them."

"That's not a bad idea," Scotty agreed. "Might make everyone feel better."

Murry grumbled, "You've got to be joking."

"You take the first shift, Kate. I'll go next, then Scotty, then Murry. That way we can all get a little sleep."

Scotty shook his head. "I doubt any of us will sleep much."

Kate had the same thought.

"You and Murry start on the tents," Rand said. "After that, move the horses. In the meantime, I'll get Kate situated in that group of shrubs up the trail."

Scotty nodded. "Will do."

Murry grumbled under his breath but jogged off without making a further fuss. Rand took hold of Kate's arm again and led her to the canopy sheltering the cooking equipment. He grabbed the flashlight off the camp stove and handed it to her.

"You may need this."

She slipped it under her poncho and into the belt of her fanny pack. They stopped beneath the other canopy and retrieved Kate's canteen from her saddlebag. She slung that over her shoulder.

"Anything else you can think of you'll need?" he asked.

"No."

They walked up the trail to the cluster of shrubs. There, they found a boulder low to the ground and up against the mountain wall. The boulder was wide enough for Kate to sit somewhat comfortably for her shift. Rand grabbed a smaller boulder and deposited it in front of the other one.

"For your feet. Keep them elevated and off the ground in case there's a strike nearby."

"The lightning looks to be far away."

"For now. Storms can move fast. Will you be warm enough?"

"I have my jacket on under my poncho."

"Are you warm enough?" he repeated more firmly.

"Yes."

"Holler if you hear or see anything. I don't care how insignificant."

"I will."

He hesitated as if reluctant to leave her. "May God watch over you, Kate."

"Thank you. And thanks for caring."

He went still for a long, tension-filled moment. Had she misspoken? Her anxiety spiked.

"I do care, Kate. While you're on this trail ride, your safety is my responsibility. But that's all there is—"

"Of course. I didn't mean to imply…"

Except she had meant to imply his concern for her was personal. She'd started to believe his anger toward her had softened. If it had, it wasn't by much. The precautions he was taking with her were no different than those he'd take with Scotty or Murry or any of the kids.

"I'll be back to swap shifts with you in a couple hours," were his parting words before he strode off to join Murry and Scotty.

Kate sat alone in the rain, staring away from camp and at the mountaintop in the direction of the gunshot. She wasn't as much watching for danger as thinking.

What had she expected? That she'd change Rand's feelings about her in one day? The quote from Romans came to mind. *But if we hope for that we see not, then do we with patience wait for it.*

Kate would wait. A week, anyway. At which point she'd leave Still Water Ranch.

"I could use some guidance about now, Lord," she murmured. "Was I wrong to come here? What plans do You have in store for me?"

Lightning flashed, thunder rolled and the wind picked up, pelting her with rain and soaking her jacket collar through the poncho's neck opening. Definitely not the answer she'd been hoping for.

Chapter Five

Rand awoke with a start. For a moment, he didn't know where he was. Water dripping in from the flap in the tent and dampening his sleeping bag reminded him, and he sat bolt upright.

Kate! Was she okay?

That she was his first thought startled him almost as much as waking up in a strange place. Rand had always made a point of thinking about Kate as little as possible.

He recalled she'd taken the first shift at guard duty, and he'd relieved her. That she'd managed to tolerate sitting for two hours on a hard boulder in the pouring, chilly rain without complaint spoke to her determination and endurance. She had as much courage as Rand or any of them.

He shouldn't have dismissed her so abruptly last night when she'd thanked him for caring. But the truth was, her remark had struck too close to home. He *had* started to care for her, and he didn't want to. He'd rather stay angry at her. There was comfort and familiarity in that emotion. He'd lived with it for ten years. Having his feelings for her change caused confusion and forced him to examine the fairness of his stance against her more closely. For that reason, and others, he'd shut her down before he said something he might regret.

Slowly, so as not to disturb the boys sharing the four-person tent with him, Rand climbed out of his sleeping bag. He grabbed his outerwear from where he'd stowed it in the corner and exited the tent. He stood beneath the tiny awning and put on his boots as best he could without getting his socks wet. After donning his jacket, poncho and cowboy hat, he made a dash in the dark toward the closest canopy. There, he retrieved a bandana from his back jeans pocket and dried off his face and hands.

While the thunder and lightning had ceased during the night, rain continued to fall in fat drops that stung when they hit bare skin. The sun had yet to rise behind the blanket of dark clouds. Rand guessed it to be after five. He'd know the exact time if he had his phone.

A glance up the trail assured him Murry remained at his post on the boulder, his dim outline hunched over. Rand was bound to be on the receiving end of a litany of complaints. He didn't care. They'd made it through the night safe and sound and with no more gunshots. That was all he cared about. Once they finished breakfast, they'd saddle up and start for home. The ride would be wet and uncomfortable, and there would be some treacherous patches along the way, but they'd make it.

A survey of the camp assured Rand no one had roused yet. He shoved his cowboy hat farther down onto his head, ducked out from under the canopy and trudged up the trail to Murry.

The wrangler stood at his approach.

"How's it going?" Rand asked.

"I think I deserve a bonus. We all do. This has been

one miserable trail ride. Was sitting out in the rain really necessary?"

"I appreciate you doing it, Murry. The kids were worried."

"Them or your girlfriend?"

The remark landed wrong. Rand wasn't in the mood. "She's not my girlfriend."

"Yeah? Could've fooled me the way you pander to her."

Rand's hackles rose, but he held his temper. Anything else would give Murry the wrong idea. "I'm going to let that remark pass. You're tired and cold and miserable. We all are."

Murry snorted with disgust. "Last time I go on one of these rides with a woman."

Rand wanted to say that Kate hadn't complained once and that *he'd* go on a ride with her any day over Murry.

"What's the problem? You seemed to like her well enough yesterday. And then what? You found out she's served time?"

"Honestly," Murry admitted, "yeah. She has a troubled past."

"So do a lot of people who come to Still Water Ranch."

"And like the rest of them, she has to earn my trust."

Rand could debate Murry. He could preach to him about the golden rule: treat others as you want to be treated. Except he'd be wasting his breath.

Instead, he asked, "What time is it?"

Murry pulled out his phone. "Almost five thirty."

"Have you tried calling the ranch yet this morning?"

"I'll do that right now." Murry dialed and smiled broadly. "It's ringing." A few seconds later, he said, "Grandpa Billy. Yeah, we're hanging in there. Rand's right here."

"Tell him we're cutting the trip short and coming home early."

Murry relayed the message, citing the rainstorm and concern over the gunshot. "Grandpa Billy says coming home early is the smart thing to do."

Immediately after that, the call dropped. Nonetheless, Rand's nerves relaxed. No more gunshots. They'd talked to Grandpa Billy. And they were heading home. All would be well soon.

Even better, the sun was rising. Pitch black had given way to a gloomy, oppressive gray. Beneath the trees, the horses stomped the ground with their hooves, nipped their neighbor and nickered. They'd missed grazing on the grass during the night and were hungry.

Together, Rand and Murry returned to the campsite. Scotty emerged from another of the tents, stretched and then joined them. A few of the kids, too. They jumped over puddles and shook wet branches at each other, soaking themselves with water in the process and laughing. The fear from the previous night had dissipated.

"Hey," Rand called to the kids. "If you have that much energy, you can help Scotty divvy up the remaining pellets between the horses and lead them to the spring for a drink when they're done eating."

All at once, Kate flew out of a tent and came running toward Rand, mindless of the bruising rain and that she wasn't wearing her jacket or poncho. Her hair, loose for a change, hung long and straight.

"Rand! Have you or anyone seen Serene and Brie?"

"What?"

"They aren't in the tent. Have you seen them?" she repeated.

"No. I just got up. Murry? Any sign of them?"

The wrangler shrugged. "Sorry."

"They must have gone to the bushes for some privacy," Rand said.

"Except all their stuff is missing." She looked around, tugging anxiously on her hair.

"Kate. You're soaked. Get your jacket and poncho on. If the girls aren't back in a few minutes, I'll go after them. They can't have gone far. Not in this weather."

"Take me with you."

"All right."

She related to the girls well, better than he did. It was a skill that might come in handy.

"Which horses were they riding?" Scotty asked.

"Flapjack and Little Red."

Scotty scrutinized the herd. "All the horses are here. The girls didn't ride off. They're on foot."

Rand hadn't liked the idea of them taking the horses. They could have been anywhere by now. He didn't like the idea of them being on foot, either.

Kate returned to her tent and came out a few minutes later fully dressed, her hair gathered into a ponytail.

By now, the rest of the kids were up and about. Rand instructed them to break camp by rolling up their sleeping bags and disassembling the tents. While he and Kate went in search of the missing foster sisters, Scotty and Murry would oversee saddling the horses and preparing a simple pancake breakfast.

Rand grabbed the pair of binoculars from his saddlebags. "You ready?"

They went fifty yards down from camp first, calling the girls' names and searching for any sign of movement. Rain pelted them with a fury. More than once, they lost their footing on the slippery ground and went down.

"Do you think they're hiding from us?" Kate asked, wiping dirt off her pants. "They are rebellious. Or Serene is, and Brie goes along with whatever she says."

"It's possible," Rand agreed. "Except I'm having trouble believing Serene would remain out in this weather a minute longer than necessary."

"Which means they could be lost."

He wasn't ready to consider that. "Let's get back to camp. If they're not there, we'll head *up* the trail this time to search for them."

"Wouldn't Murry have seen them if they went in that direction? They'd have walked right past him."

"Unless they went off the trail and cut behind him. He wouldn't have heard over the noise of the storm."

"But why?"

"Your guess is as good as mine." He couldn't help wondering if there was a connection to his missing phone.

"What if they're hurt?"

The thought had also occurred to Rand. "Don't worry. We'll find them."

At camp, they learned the girls still hadn't returned.

"Did Serene or Brie say anything to any of you?" Kate asked the group of kids. "You're not squealing on them, and you won't get in trouble for answering." When no one responded, she pleaded. "This is important. We have to find them."

"I heard them leave the tent," Aiesha admitted. "But they didn't say anything. Not to me."

"What time was that?"

"I don't know. It was dark out, for sure. An hour ago?"

More like two. Before Rand had woken up. He tried

not to let the kids or Kate see his growing concern and concentrated on finding Serene and Brie.

"Scotty," he said. "Come help me and Kate saddle our horses and the girls'. We'll cover ground faster and have a better view on horseback. Then, when we find the girls, we can all ride out."

"Maybe I should go with you," Scotty said. "In case you need…" He let the sentence drop.

Rand mentally finished it for him. Someone stronger because the girls were in a jam or had run off. The suggestion had merit. Except, if the girls were reluctant to return, Kate would be the one to talk some sense into them.

"Thanks. We'll be all right." He glanced at her and read the fear in her eyes. He almost reached out a hand to reassure her but didn't.

"You both be careful," Scotty said. He was keeping up a brave front for the kids, but his cheer wasn't fooling Rand.

"Why don't you grab some breakfast," Rand told Kate and motioned to Murry, who was cooking up pancakes beneath the canopy.

"I'll eat when we return with the girls," she insisted and headed toward where the horses were tied.

Before long, they were mounted and ready to start their search. Kate followed Rand, leading Flapjack and Little Red behind her, one tied to the other.

"Can you handle both horses?" he asked.

"No problem."

"We'll be packed and ready to hit the trail when you return," Scotty called after them.

Rand and Kate traversed the steep, slick trail, calling out for the girls every few minutes. At a level spot, they stopped to let the horses catch their breath. Rand raised the binoculars to his eyes and turned his head in a slow circle. Rain blurred his view, colors melting into one another. On his second pass, he spotted a flash of yellow fifty yards off the trail near a rocky rise that jutted from the ground like the back of a dragon.

"Wait! I see something." He dried off the binoculars on his jacket and looked again. No doubt about it. The moving flash of yellow could only be a rain poncho. Relief swept over him. "I think it's them. One of them, at least."

Behind him, Kate released a soft sob. "Thank God."

They turned off the trail, pushing their mounts hard across the rough, uneven terrain. More than once, the horses stumbled, their hooves sinking into the drenched earth.

Rand called for the girls. "Serene. Brie."

"Over here," came Brie's faint reply.

Rand murmured a quiet, "Thank You, Lord," before glancing backward at Kate.

She didn't see him. She'd lifted her face heavenward and closed her eyes, not seeming to mind the rain striking her face. He didn't disturb her, once again marveling at her courage and determination. Riding up the mountain in this storm while leading two horses was no small feat.

A moment later, he started forward, Kate behind him. As they neared Brie, she waved her arms over her head. "Hurry."

Where was Serene? Rand hoped she hadn't injured herself. The ravine opposite the rise fell straight down a dizzying six stories. It was dotted by treacherous rocky ledges that, upon impact, could crush bones, split a skull open or slice through flesh.

Rand reined Mega Max to a stop and climbed off. Crippling pain shot up his legs, a result of the cold weather and sitting at length in the saddle combining with his lingering nerve damage. He held on to his saddle horn until he could take a step without dropping to his knees.

Kate appeared beside him. "Are you okay?"

"Yeah."

She didn't press him for more, which he appreciated, and waited until he was able to walk.

Brie met them halfway, breathless from the jaunt and red-faced. "You're here."

"What in the world were you thinking?" Rand demanded, sharper than he'd intended. "You put not only yourselves in danger, but Kate and me, too."

The girl was on the verge of tears. "I'm sorry. I'm so, so sorry. I know we're in trouble."

"We'll talk about that later." He was certain her foster sister had masterminded this little adventure, so he didn't hold Brie entirely responsible. Though she did need to learn to stand up for herself. It was something they tried to teach many of the youth camp members who often succumbed to peer pressure. "Let's just get home. Where's Serene?"

"In there." Brie pointed to what Rand now realized was a cave.

He released Mega Max's reins. The horse was well trained and wouldn't wander off. Kate also dismounted. Unlike Rand, she exercised caution and kept a firm grasp on her reins, maintaining control of all three horses.

With Brie tagging after him, he stooped and entered the cave. There wasn't enough room for him to stand, and he waited, hunched over, for his eyes to adjust to the darkness. "Serene?"

"What?"

The girl crouched on the floor near the opening, not bothering to hide the fact she had Rand's phone.

No, that was wrong. She perched on a campstool. It was then Rand noticed the cave's contents. Someone was using it to store gear. Crates and bins were stacked against the far wall. A dilapidated two-by-four folding table held several boxes, both the cardboard and plastic variety. A pair of coolers had been tucked beneath the table and a blue plastic tarp covered a collection of boxy shapes on the ground.

"Let's go, Serene."

She glared at the phone. "I need to make a call, and I can't figure out your stupid pass code."

The girl had a stubborn streak a mile wide. How she'd managed to drag herself and Brie this far during a storm, and past an unsuspecting Murry, was something else. He almost admired her moxie. Too bad she couldn't apply herself positively instead of always getting into trouble.

Rand grumbled to himself. She was going home after this prank. He didn't care how much she protested.

"Enough, Serene. We can't stay here."

She curled protectively around the phone. "I just need to make one call."

"Either you come now," Rand said, his tone like steel, "or I'll carry you out of here."

Serene huffed and stood, though she had to duck, too, or else hit her head. They went outside. By then, the starch had left her. When he held out his hand, she reluctantly surrendered the phone.

"All this for what?" Rand made a sound of disgust. "To call a friend or some boy?"

"My mom," she said, so soft Rand almost didn't hear her.

"Your mom?"

"You wouldn't understand." The raised chin and defiant spark in her eyes had returned.

"Try me."

"I need to make sure she's all right."

"You could have asked to use my phone."

"I didn't want to have to explain why." She wiped at her nose with the back of her hand.

"Explain what?" Rand's patience was at an end.

"My dad sometimes…he…he isn't nice to my mom when I'm gone."

"Serene." His anger instantly evaporated, replaced with sorrow. This could explain why Serene was in foster care. "Does your dad hurt your mom?"

"I have to call her," she repeated, a note of desperation in her voice.

"All right. You will. I promise. But first, I'm calling Scotty and Murry. You wait with Ms. Kate and Brie."

She trudged over to where Kate and Brie stood by the horses. Brie gave her foster sister a hug, and for the first time, Rand wondered if she let Serene boss her around as her way of being supportive.

Funny how you could misread a situation. His glance went briefly to Kate. He may have been quick to judge her, in the past and now.

For the first time ever, he considered the three teenage boys who'd cut the straps on his saddle and wondered if something other than mean-spiritedness had driven them to do what they had. What if his rival had lived with an addict or abusive parent and lashed out at others in response? What if he'd been under intense pressure to win by a competitive dad? Or desperately needed the prize money?

Rand had believed only that they were cruel, not that they'd chosen poorly because of extenuating circumstances. The last he'd heard a few years ago, they were long out of prison and leading law-abiding lives.

It was something to think about. And he would when they got home.

Shielding his phone from the rain, he unlocked the display with his fingerprint and called Scotty. The wrangler answered on the third ring.

"We found them," Rand said.

"Thank God."

"We should be back to you in about an hour."

"Better get after it. We got us a problem. Cayden took a nasty tumble. Fell about fifteen feet."

"What!"

"He's hurt, Rand. Busted arm and a couple of ribs for sure. Possible concussion. Kid's trying to be brave, but he's hurtin'."

"You need to get him out of there."

"Ansel called to have the kid flown out, but the medical copter can't reach us here. Too iffy in this storm. We're going to ride to where the trail junctions with the one to the ruins. There's a wide, flat spot there. Poor kid'll be miserable. Nothing else we can do."

"Don't wait on us," Rand insisted. "Kate and I can bring the girls out. You and Murry just get Cayden to the helicopter and the rest of the kids to the trailhead. We'll meet you there. Like I said, we're an hour behind you."

"Will do, buddy."

Guilt ate at Rand as he disconnected. He should have canceled the trail ride. Didn't matter that there'd only been a fifty-fifty chance of rain when they left. As soon as it had started to sprinkle yesterday, he should have turned them around and headed back. This was all his fault.

He motioned Serene over, used his fingerprint to open his phone and gave it to her. "Five minutes," he said. "Then we leave."

"Five minutes?" she whined.

"Take it or leave it."

The area may be deserted now, but there was no guarantee the owners of the cave supplies wouldn't suddenly return and not be happy to find a group of trespassers.

Rand listened while Serene spoke with her mother. From her side of the conversation, it sounded as if her mom was fine. That, or she was lying because she didn't want to worry her daughter.

"Rand?"

He glanced up to see Kate. She'd left Brie in charge of the horses. "Everything okay?"

She knitted her brows with concern. "I'm not sure."

"What is it?"

"I found this on the ground." She opened her closed fist to reveal a brass bullet casing. It appeared brand-new, as if recently fired from a gun.

In his mind, he heard the gunshot from last night.

"I think we need to leave," Kate said. "Right away."

"Give me a minute."

She was right, they did need to leave. But Rand had

to confirm his suspicions if only so he could correctly report what they'd found to the local authorities, or they might not take him seriously.

He returned to the cave and flipped open the first crate within reach. It was filled with explosives, according to the labels on the boxes. A nearby bin contained ammunition. He lifted the plastic tarp enough to reveal several five-gallon cans of gasoline, a portable generator and a collection of mining equipment including jackhammers, picks, shovels and safety gear.

He hurried out of the cave, his leg muscles on fire. "Finish your call right now," he told Serene, who glared at him. He ignored her and went to Kate.

Seeing him, she paled. "What did you find?"

"We've stumbled onto an illegal mining operation."

Chapter Six

"It's pouring," Serene grumbled. "Why can't we wait in the cave?"

Kate and Rand had agreed not to tell the girls about the gun casing and illegal mining until they were safely away. Unfortunately, there were consequences to their plan. Unaware of the potential danger, Serene kept procrastinating about leaving.

"We'll be back to camp half an hour tops," Kate reasoned, refastening the chin strap on her horse's bridle.

Brie stood next to Little Red, stroking the horse's neck. "Is Cayden going to be all right?"

"He should be. Once the helicopter gets him to the nearest hospital." Kate prayed the boy would be fine and was glad Rand had instructed Scotty to start without them. Cayden's well-being took priority. And, like Rand, she was confident they'd make it down the mountain no problem. As long as they were gone before the illegal miners returned.

Rand untied the lead rope connecting Little Red to Flapjack. "Mount up, girls."

He wasn't doing a good job hiding his anxiety.

"I don't see what the big deal is." Serene crossed her arms over her middle. "No one will be at camp when we arrive anyway."

"Scotty and Murry and Mr. Laurent have enough to worry about with Cayden," Kate said. "We aren't going to add to their burdens by being late."

"Okay, okay." Serene rolled her eyes.

Kate ignored her. The girl's small outbursts were the result of her wishing she could be home with her mother.

The horses had been on their best behavior, waiting patiently. Brie stuck her left foot in the stirrup and swung her right leg up and over the saddle. Serene gathered her horse's reins, which were wet and slick. Kate waited on the girls in case they needed assistance.

With no warning, and much too close for comfort, a loud explosion sounded on the other side of the mountain behind the cave. Kate gasped and instinctively cowered, holding tight on to her startled horse.

"What was th—" Serene didn't get the chance to finish her question.

"Hit the ground, everyone," Rand hollered.

A second explosion shattered the air.

He rushed toward Kate. After that, everything happened at once—too fast for her to process. Serene screamed and dropped to her knees. Little Red whinnied and reared, knocking Brie off. The girl hit her head when she landed and cried out. Flapjack kicked, his rear hoof missing Rand by mere inches. With a squeal, Little Red started galloping toward the trail, her feet sending mud flying into the air.

Kate's horse jerked back, ripping the reins from her grasp. He and the other horses galloped away in the same direction as Little Red, bucking and kicking.

Kate went after them, yelling, "Whoa, whoa! Come back."

A third explosion sounded. She swore the ground shifted beneath her feet.

No, not the ground. Rand had grabbed her by the arm and yanked her to a stop.

"You can't catch them. You'll just exhaust yourself trying."

She watched the horses disappear down the trail, a weary sigh escaping her. What else could go wrong on this trip?

"They won't go far," Rand said. "Chances are we'll find them on the trail."

He and Kate returned to check on the girls. Both were distraught but otherwise all right. Brie would have a few lumps and bruises to show off and a story to tell when they got home. And they would get home. Kate had faith.

Dear Lord in heaven, please watch over us.

"Were those bombs?" Serene demanded.

"I don't know," Kate hedged.

"And we're not sticking around to find out." Rand fished out his phone and pressed a speed dial number, only to groan in frustration. "I'm not getting a signal." Stuffing the phone in his pocket, he started walking, his gaze on the ominous sky. "I vote we get out of here."

He turned, and his foot went into a hole. The next instant, he face-planted in a patch of low-growing shrubs.

Kate hurried toward him. "Rand! Are you okay?"

"Yeah." He struggled to sit up. Fortunately, his jacket and rain poncho had protected him against the worst of the shrubs' pointy thorns.

"You sure?"

He waved off the hand she offered and got to his

feet, each movement visibly causing him pain. She left him to his own devices, refusing to embarrass him or injure his pride by insisting on helping. Instead, she retrieved his phone, which had landed several feet away. The black screen was shattered.

"Give it to me," he said.

Wordlessly, Kate handed him the phone. He pressed the power button. Twice. The screen remained black. Grumbling under his breath, he shoved the useless phone into his jacket pocket. "You have yours, right?"

"I do," Kate said. "In my fanny pack."

"We need to call Scotty or Murry."

"Later. Once we're on the trail."

By then, Serene and Brie had joined them.

"What are we gonna do without the horses?" Serene lamented.

"Walk," Rand said.

"In the rain?"

"You walked here."

His remark silenced the girl, and the four of them fell into line.

Halfway to the trail, they heard the distant sound of an engine. Kate's glance cut to Rand, and she instantly knew they had the same thought: the illegal miners were returning.

He motioned. "This way."

They each grabbed one of the girls and started running toward the trail. Though less than a hundred feet away, the distance seemed to stretch for miles. Rocks and holes created an obstacle course. Kate and Brie, their arms locked, stumbled every third step.

The noise of the engine grew louder and more threatening.

"We need to hide!" Kate said.

Rand changed direction. They dove behind a cluster of bushes just as an ATV carrying a lone driver appeared over the rise.

"Don't move," Rand ordered in a harsh whisper. "Don't talk. No matter what happens."

"Maybe he can give us a ride back to camp," Serene said, disregarding Rand's instructions.

"He's part of an illegal mining operation. Now, be quiet before he decides to shoot first and ask questions later."

"Really?"

"Be quiet. I'm serious, Serene."

Brie began to whimper.

Through the veil of branches, Kate watched as the ATV stopped in front of the cave entrance. Leaving the engine idling, the driver dismounted and disappeared inside. A minute later, he reappeared and began searching the area.

"What's he looking for?" Kate whispered to Rand.

"I think the better question is what did he find?"

Chills skittered up her spine.

Even from a distance, and with their view partially obscured, the man appeared large and menacing. A long ponytail snaked out from beneath his helmet. The black visor hid his features, except for a full, scruffy beard that must have taken him years to grow. He wore a stained and tattered canvas coat, heavy work boots and green cargo pants. The pelting rain had no effect on his aggressive prowl as he inspected the area in an ever-widening semicircle.

"He's found our footprints and the hoofprints," Rand said.

"What will he do?"

The question was answered before Kate drew in her next shallow breath. The man raised his head and, she swore, stared directly at them. Had he spotted their yellow rain ponchos?

The man climbed onto the ATV and revved the engine. Her fervent prayers for safety were answered, for instead of heading toward them, he executed a U-turn and sped off.

"We don't have much time," Rand said and pulled Serene to her feet. "He's going to report what he found to his partners. We have to hurry."

Kate helped Brie to stand.

"If we head to the trail, and he comes looking for us," Kate said, her voice trembling, "we won't stand a chance."

Rand pointed. "Let's take cover behind those boulders."

They all started running. Brie began to cry in earnest.

"Shut up," Serene snapped at her foster sister.

"Enough," Kate told her. "We're all scared."

The boulders, some of them three feet tall and just as wide, formed a natural barrier. Kate wondered if Rand would be able to climb over them. Frankly, she wasn't sure she and the girls could make it over, either.

He surprised her. Fueled by adrenaline or fear, he managed better than expected. Once over, he helped Serene and Brie.

"Get down," he ordered.

They immediately obeyed.

Kate was halfway across the boulders when he grabbed her, depositing her beside him. He didn't release her right away.

"Are you okay?" he asked.

"Yes. Are you?"

He nodded, finally letting her go.

Kate crouched, Brie on one side of her, Serene on the other and Rand on the outside—first in the line of fire should the miners come after them. They made themselves as small as possible and waited. For ten minutes, nothing happened. The man on the ATV didn't reappear.

"Are we safe?" Serene asked.

"Too soon to say," Kate answered before Rand could.

Another ten minutes passed. Brie shivered and Serene squirmed. Rand reached over Serene to give Kate's arm a reassuring squeeze.

She was just starting to wonder if they might be in the clear when the sound of an engine sent her pulse into hyperdrive.

"He's coming back," Brie cried out and rose. "He's going to kill us."

Kate grabbed for the girl, but she was too fast and scurried away to where the boulders met the mountainside.

"Brie." Kate followed behind the girl, crawling on all fours. "Come back. He'll see you."

Suddenly, Brie came to a halt. She sat back on her calves, covered her mouth and screamed.

Kate came up behind her, ready to slap a hand over the girl's mouth and drag her back to the others.

Brie appeared not to notice her and screamed again. And again.

The next instant, Kate saw what had sent the girl over the edge.

A body lay crumpled on the ground, the face dirty and discolored, the eyes lifeless. The mouth hung open in a silent plea.

Despite the gruesome appearance, Kate recognized

the man and the clothes he wore—the hiker from yesterday who, along with his companion, had stopped on the trail to talk to them.

Kate pressed a fist to her lips as bile rose in her throat. With her other hand, she pulled Brie away and hugged her close.

If Rand didn't do something right now, they'd be discovered by the man on the ATV. Likely, Brie's screams had been covered by the raging storm, and maybe the miner's thickly padded helmet.

Rand half crawled, half scrambled to where Kate and Brie huddled next to—what? Blinking, he wiped rainwater from his eyes and peered over Kate's shoulder. Shock rippled through him at the pair of lifeless eyes staring at him from a sickeningly gray face. The only dead person he'd ever seen was his grandfather, nestled peacefully in his casket and wearing his Sunday suit. He'd looked nothing like this man.

This man. The hiker. Rand had recognized him instantly. Dear God.

The downpour hadn't washed away a large, dark stain on the front of his jacket. Blood.

Where was his companion, the woman? Rand looked around. He didn't see a second body.

"What's happening?" Serene asked from behind him.

He moved to block her view of the body. "Stay where you are."

"Is Brie okay?"

Not to dismiss her concerns, but Rand couldn't deal with Serene's drama right now. Their lives depended on what happened next. "Kate, are you all right?"

"Yes," she answered in a wobbly voice.

At least Brie had stopped screaming, though she sobbed and clung to Kate.

"You've got to quiet her," he said.

"Brie, honey." Kate hugged the girl closer. "We're in danger. Big danger. You have to pull yourself together."

Her frank tone had the desired effect. Brie slowly calmed.

Rand peered between two boulders. The man had stopped searching the area in front of the cave and was again seated on the ATV. He was talking on a phone. No, a handheld radio of some kind. Which meant he wasn't alone and, more than likely, his partners were in the vicinity. If they returned and came looking for Rand, Kate and the girls, there would be five dead bodies.

Rand refused to consider such a gruesome outcome. Were they far enough away and well hidden? Unlikely. They'd be spotted within moments if the man decided to check on the body, which he might. Rand sent God a prayer, asking Him to direct the man away and give them the opportunity to escape.

Again, Rand wondered what had happened to the hiker's companion. Was she also dead or had she escaped? Maybe the illegal miners were holding her captive.

Rand's stomach clenched at the thought of Kate and the girls helpless and vulnerable at the hands of killers. More than ever, he needed to get them to safety. He shifted, hating the nerve damage in his legs and that he couldn't run fast. At this rate, he'd be more of a hindrance than a help.

Please, Lord, give me strength to shepherd Kate and the girls to a safe haven.

Suddenly, a giant streak of lightning cut across the

horizon and illuminated the entire sky. Two seconds later, thunder cracked, loud enough that Kate jerked, Brie yelped and Serene grabbed Rand's arm.

"Are we gonna die?"

"Absolutely not," he assured her, not liking the thought of the four of them traveling the trail on foot and in the open. Perhaps they should wait here behind the boulders.

But for how long? All day? The storm was worsening by the minute. As if to prove it, the skies opened up and released a torrent of rain. Drops the size of pebbles assaulted them with a vicious force.

The downpour must have been too much for the man on the ATV, for he executed a sharp U-turn and drove off the way he'd come.

Rand made a snap decision. He grabbed Kate by the arm. "We need to get out of here while we can."

"What about him?" Her glance cut to the dead hiker.

"There's nothing we can do. As soon as we're able to, we'll report his location to the authorities and inform them of the illegal mining operation."

"Him, who?" Serene tried to see around Rand.

In hindsight, he should have told her about the hiker. "Serene, not now."

"Is he dead?" She let out a gasp, and then shrieked.

Rand put a hand on her shoulder and repeated, "Not now, Serene."

She began to shiver. "I'm scared."

"We're going to be okay." He turned to Kate. "We can't delay."

She nodded and gathered Brie's hands in hers. "You stick right beside me. Okay?"

Brie nodded.

"Same with you," Rand told Serene. "Stay together. No taking off on your own. Got it?"

"I promise."

For once, the girl complied without resistance. If only she'd obeyed that rule to begin with, they wouldn't be in this predicament. He hoped that when she was home with her mom or in the care of her foster parents, she'd look back and learn a lesson from the experience.

He pushed up to a half-crouching position, gritting his teeth at what felt like ribbons of fire shooting up his legs. The trail was a good thirty yards away. As if the obstacle course created by mesquite trees, cacti, thick brush, rocks and potholes wasn't difficult enough to navigate, the ground to the right of the trail fell sharply away at a dizzying angle.

They'd have to be fast, agile and relentless if they were to get far enough away before being spotted. If the man came down the trail after them, they'd be sitting ducks. And he clearly had no qualms about shooting intruders.

Five minutes. That was all the time they needed. Four hundred heartbeats. A hundred breaths. Seventy steps. They could do it.

One by one, they stood and inched their way out from behind the wall of boulders, Rand in the lead. He kept an eye out for any ATVs. No one looked back at the dead hiker.

Emerging from behind the boulders in single file, they headed straight toward the trail—running as fast as they were able in their sodden boots.

"Faster," Rand urged.

When Brie tripped over a rock, Kate caught her and righted her without stopping. Rand misstepped and collided with a prickly pear cactus. He grunted in pain as sharp needles penetrated his clothing and pierced his skin. Determined not to slow their progress, he struggled to his feet. When Kate extended a hand to him, he took it.

"I'm okay," he said before she could ask. "Let's keep going."

Serene took the lead after that, her eyes bright with fear.

Rain beat down on them, obscuring their vision and impeding their progress. Lightning flashed. Thunder clapped. The wind did its best to knock them off course.

Instinct alone led them toward their destination. The trail loomed ahead, coming closer but not fast enough. How many minutes had passed?

"Wait," Brie cried out and bent over, clutching her middle. "I can't go on."

"Don't stop." Kate grabbed her and dragged her along.

Rand's lungs burned. His legs throbbed. A cramp stabbed him in the side with crippling intensity.

Still, he pushed on—until the whine of an engine penetrated the roar of the storm.

He slowed and turned to see the man on the ATV returning. Fear nearly drove him to his knees. There was no place to hide, no escape route. No way to outrun a motorized vehicle and no protection against a bullet. But to give up was a guaranteed death sentence.

"Keep running!" he hollered.

If they reached the trail, they could jump over the steep edge and slide down to the ravine at the bottom. Risky, yes. Someone could get hurt. But the ravine was too steep for the ATV to follow without crashing. The driver would be forced to either turn back or attempt to go around, the route taking him a half mile out of the way.

That wouldn't prevent him from firing on them. Bullets could travel down a steep ravine no problem.

What other chance did they have except to try?

Close. They were almost there. Another fifteen feet to the trail.

And, then, the ATV was upon them. The engine sounded like the roar of an angry beast. The smell of gasoline filled his nostrils and seared his throat. A few more seconds, and the man would mow them down.

"Rand?" Kate's fingers crushed his.

"I've got you." He ground to a stop and pulled her close. He opened his other arm to Serene and Brie, who scrambled to huddle against him. "Shh. It's all right. We'll be fine." He had to believe that. They would not wind up like the dead hiker.

The girls whimpered. Kate shook. Rand fought to contain his spiraling thoughts. He had to stay in control.

The ATV stopped in front of them, too far for Rand to charge the driver and overtake him. Not that he could. The gun in the man's hand pointing straight at them stopped Rand cold.

The LORD is on my side; I will not fear: what can man do unto me?

He silently repeated the words from the Psalm over and over.

The driver stood and, leaving the engine idling, dismounted. He never took the gun off them. With his free hand, he lifted the visor on his helmet. A pair of dark eyes studied them. Thin lips curved up in an evil grin.

"Well," he said as casually as if he'd come upon them in the aisle of a grocery store. "I'd tell you to hold it right there, but it seems you already have." And then he barked a laugh.

Chapter Seven

Kate had never been more frightened in her life. Even the day she'd been carted off to prison didn't compare to this. Then, she hadn't known what to expect. Today, the end of her life stood in front of her, wearing a grimy canvas coat and a black helmet, and aiming a gun at her.

Her insides seized, and her limbs trembled. She focused on Rand's arm around her shoulder. She would not die alone. The thought was both comforting and frightening. She didn't want anyone else to lose their life.

The man advanced, his black eyes drilling into her. "Well, well, well. Lookie there. A woman. And pretty at that."

Kate went rigid with fear at the thought of his intentions for her. And what about the hiker's companion? She wasn't at the campsite, but that meant nothing.

Straining, Kate listened for more engines. It wouldn't be long before the other illegal miners arrived. Would the man wait for them or take matters into his own hands?

"Don't hurt us," Serene pleaded, her voice that of a small child's. She held on to Brie, who swayed unsteadily.

Tears spilled from Kate's eyes, only to be washed away by the rain.

They're young and innocent. They don't deserve this. I beg You, Lord, please spare them.

Rand's tortured glance met hers. His arm around her tightened, letting her know he wouldn't abandon them. She was grateful to him and tried to convey as much.

"We don't want any trouble," Rand said to the man.

He chuckled. "A little too late for that, pal."

"Let us go. We won't tell anyone. I promise."

"Oh, you're not going to tell. I'll see to that."

All trace of humor vanished. The man's malevolent glare landed on Kate. This couldn't be happening. She thought of her family. Would they miss her? Stop being angry at her? All at once, she wanted to see them again. To die without saying goodbye was too much to bear.

"I'll do whatever you want," Rand said. "Just let the rest of them go."

"No." The objection erupted from Kate's mouth.

"Well, isn't that sweet?" The man chuckled again. "Don't worry, darling. None of you are leaving."

"They can't identify you," Rand continued, attempting to reason with their captor. "They don't know these mountains and can't lead anyone back here. You could be long gone by then."

The man pretended to consider. "Don't think my partners will like that much. And, besides, there's too much at stake for us to leave. Like the old saying goes, there's gold in them there hills."

He was enjoying this. The idea sickened Kate to her core.

"Release the girls," she blurted. "Take me instead. But please just let them go."

The man's features darkened. "How about instead you give me your phones? Can't have people tracking your GPS."

"We have only one," Rand said. "And it's broken."

"Nice try. But I'm not stupid."

Kate glanced at Rand. He nodded, cut his eyes to her waist and then back to the man. He was trying to tell her something, but what? To go along and hand over her phone?

Moving slowly, she unzipped her fanny pack. By then, Rand had his phone out.

"Toss 'em here." The man indicated the ground in front of his feet.

Rand obeyed, his broken phone landing several feet short of its mark. "Kate," he murmured, almost too softly for her to hear.

She suddenly understood. With shaking fingers, she tossed her phone. It, too, intentionally fell short.

The man glared at them. "You're joking."

No one moved.

"The brats' phones, too."

"They don't have any," Rand said.

"How about I search them and see for myself?"

"No," Serene cried out. She and Brie cowered behind Kate.

"I promise you," Rand said, his jaw working, his words terse. "They don't have phones. There's no need to search them."

The man studied him, then abruptly smiled. "Doesn't matter anyway."

What did that mean? Kate moved to further shield the girls.

The man crushed the two phones beneath the heel of his boot and then kicked them under a bush.

She watched, desperately wishing she'd made a call when they'd first heard the engine. Would Scotty or Murry come looking for them when they didn't arrive at the trailhead? What were the chances they'd be found alive?

With the phones demolished, the man pointed his gun at Rand. "You first, I reckon."

He was going to kill them! Kate's heart lurched inside her chest. "No! Don't."

The girls screamed.

"Rand." Kate began to weep. "I'm sorry. I'm so sorry."

Rand murmured something unintelligible.

She stared blankly at him.

"The pepper spray," he mouthed, his expression intent and begging her to understand.

Could she do it? If she failed, she would surely die. They'd all die, and their bodies would join the hiker's hidden behind the boulders.

She turned to face the man, who now stood only a few feet away. They had one desperate chance, and she took it.

Breaking free from the girls, she kicked at the wet ground and sent a large clump of dirt at him. Rand did the same. His aim was better, and a shower of dirt hit the man in the face.

It wasn't much. Hardly a defense. But enough to distract the man. Kate acted fast and grabbed the pepper spray from her fanny pack.

"What the—" The man shook his head, dislodging the dirt that had struck him. "You two are pathetic."

He took a step toward her. Kate raised the canister,

flipped the release and, walking toward him, fired a long stream directly at his eyes.

"Hey!" He stumbled backward and covered his face with his arms, holding the gun above his head now.

Afraid the rain might dilute the pepper spray, Kate advanced closer. Pressing the trigger on the canister with all her might, she held it a foot from the miner's face. He let out an angry cry and twisted sideways. The next second, the spray fizzled to a stop. Kate had emptied the canister.

Rand charged the man like an NFL defensive lineman. Locking his arms around the man's waist, he shoved the man down and fell on top of him.

Yelling in agony, the man tried to push Rand off and slide out from under him. If the pepper spray had done its job, his eyes and skin must be on fire, his nose and throat burning. And he may be temporarily blinded.

Still, he held on to his weapon. Rand grabbed the man's wrist in both hands and squeezed, attempting to pry the gun loose. The man bucked like a wild bronc, screaming vile names.

"Do something," Serene yelled.

Kate didn't think. She rushed over and kicked the man in the side with the toe of her boot. He let out a low "Oomph" but continued to fight. She kicked him again, harder. The man's hold on the gun weakened enough that Rand was able to rip it away. The instant he rolled off, the man clawed at his reddened face, yowling and writhing in agony.

Rand struggled to sit up. "Run!"

"Not without you."

"Kate."

She grabbed his hand and hauled him to his feet. It

was like lifting a heavy anchor from the ocean's depths. Rand's legs buckled before finally bearing his weight. When he stood, facing her, their gazes held.

"You don't listen very well, do you?" he said.

"We're in this together." She meant every word.

"All right." He looked at her, really looked, as if seeing her for the very first time. "Together."

A giant weight lifted from Kate's shoulders. They were going to get away. All of them.

Rand shoved the gun into the waistband of his jeans. His glance cut to the man thrashing on the ground. "We'd better go. The effects of the pepper spray won't last forever."

"Wait." Kate removed her pocketknife from her fanny pack and stabbed one of the ATV's tires in the sidewall over and over. Air seeped out. "Okay, now."

Like before, they each took charge of one of the girls. Already, their former captor was attempting to sit up. He'd contact his partners before long. Why hadn't they thought to confiscate his radio? Too late now.

They ran for the trail, stumbling in their haste. Above them, lightning flashed, and thunder cracked. Rain pummeled them. They'd need to find cover soon. From the storm and the miners.

Something didn't feel right to Kate. Instinct was leading them to the trail. It was the way back, after all. Yet, her instincts weren't convinced it was the safest route.

"Are you sure we're not walking into a trap?" she asked when they paused to catch their breath.

Serene and Brie stood huddled together, their expressions terrified.

"What do you mean?" Rand held on to a tree branch, his chest heaving.

"They're going to look for us on the trail." Kate covered her head with the poncho hood and fastened the snap beneath her chin. She'd lost her hat on the trail. Rand's had fallen off when he tackled the man.

"It's too steep and narrow for the ATVs," he said.

"That won't stop them. They'll follow on foot."

"We could head down the ravine."

"That's the first place they'll look for us," Kate countered. "And if they go around, they'll catch up to us in no time. Then we'll be trapped."

He considered before nodding. "You're right."

"We should go high."

"You and the girls go high," Rand said. "I'm not sure I can make it."

"You have to."

"Kate."

"We aren't leaving you," she repeated.

"Hey, everyone!" Serene straightened and pointed. "Are those our horses?"

There, a mile down the trail, four brown, black and gray spots emerged from behind a stand of trees, lumbering slowly in a group.

"We have to hurry." Serene grabbed Kate's arm.

"No," Kate said.

"What! Are you crazy?"

"The horses can't outrun the ATVs."

"But they can go places the ATVs can't," Rand countered.

"If we spotted our horses," Kate said, "so will the miners. They'll come after us. And unless we can cover a mile faster than an ATV, we don't stand a chance of reaching the horses before they get to us."

Rand blew out a long breath, clearly torn.

"Those miners aren't going to let us walk away," she said. "They're coming after us and they have the advantage. We have to be smart and stay one step ahead of them."

"By going high," Rand said.

"We'll find a place to take shelter."

"And then what?" Brie asked.

"We wait," Kate answered. "When they can't find us, they'll leave, and we head back."

Rand shook his head. "They won't abandon their operation."

"Then we hold up while they search and travel at night."

"That's a really stupid plan," Serene bit out. "We're going to die."

"The only way we'll die is if we stay here arguing or if we walk right into their hands. By going high, we have a chance."

Serene needed more convincing. "What about food and water?"

"That's the least of our problems." Kate held her balled fists at her sides. "I can't explain it—I just know that continuing on the trail is dangerous."

"Kate—"

She cut Rand off. "I've spent the last decade surviving by my wits. I've been in tight spots. We have to keep moving, and we have to stay out of sight. Our lives depend on it."

Above the din of the rain came the dreaded sound of an engine. One or more? It was too far away to tell.

"Rand. Please. Trust me."

"All right," he conceded. "I spotted a cave on the ride here yesterday. Maybe we can find it."

The engine grew louder. They didn't have a moment to waste.

"This way." Rand left the trail and started climbing the steep mountainside, grabbing boulders and branches to pull himself up.

"You two go next." Kate nudged Brie.

The climbing was difficult. Five minutes in and Kate's muscles were screaming. Her palms bled from grabbing whatever was within reach. Her knees ached. She could only imagine how much agony Rand must be in.

"Get down," he said. "Hide!"

They dropped to the ground among the brush and cacti just as three ATVs drove along the bottom of the ravine a hundred yards below. Garbed in dark outerwear and their heads hidden by coal-black helmets, the sight of them moving with purpose and carrying rifles propelled a teeth-chattering chill through Kate.

From where they lay on the ground, Rand turned toward Kate, his features pulled into a tight grimace. They were thinking the same thing. Had they gone down the ravine as he'd suggested, they'd be at this moment facing three heavily armed and proven killers with one gun to defend themselves.

"My neck hurts, and I'm cold," Brie said.

Serene scrubbed her face with her hands. "There's dirt in my eyes."

Rand felt sorry for the girls. His neck also hurt, and hunger had gnawed a hole in his stomach. His legs and hands were numb.

They hadn't moved from their spot on the ground for well over an hour. The illegal miners on the ATVs had made a total of four passes back and forth along the bottom of the ravine. At one point, they'd gotten off the ATVs and searched the surrounding area on foot. Rand had thought surely he and the girls would be spotted.

God must have been watching over them, for eventually the men climbed back on their ATVs and drove away. That was no guarantee the coast was clear or that they could resume their climb up the mountain. The miners might return at any moment and likely would.

"Do you think it's safe yet?" Kate asked.

"Let's wait a little longer."

All at once, another sound traveled toward them from behind the nearest mountain. Rand's pulse soared. It wasn't an engine but rather a distinctive *thump, thump, thump.*

"Is that a helicopter?" Kate levered herself up on to one elbow.

Rand did, too. "My guess is it's the medical transport for Cayden."

"We're saved!" Serene exclaimed as the helicopter came into view and circled to the west. She scrambled to her knees and raised her arms over her head.

Kate tugged her down. "They aren't coming this way. And you'll only alert the miners to our location."

"You're wrong!" The girl's eyes flashed.

"She's not." Rand understood the girl's desperation. He wanted the helicopter to fly this way, too. "Sorry, kiddo."

"No!" Serene collapsed onto the ground and broke into wracking sobs.

Kate rubbed her back. "I know you're scared and frustrated. But we have to be cautious if we're going to get out of here alive. Which we will. I promise."

"I don't believe you." The girl rolled away from her.

"Faith is our best weapon against those who would harm us."

"That's not true. I tried believing my dad would stop hurting my mom, but he keeps doing it."

Rand didn't blame Serene for the anger she felt or her struggles with faith. He'd been in a similar place after his accident.

"Before long, you'll be home and helping your mom," Kate soothed. "Just picture your foster parents coming to pick you up at Still Water Ranch and then taking you to visit your mom. Hold on to that image. Same for you, Brie." She patted the other girl's arm.

Rand pictured it, too. He saw the four of them meeting up with search and rescue workers or friendly hikers with a working phone. They could do this, he told himself. They could escape the illegal miners. Kate had been right about them staying together and going high.

Now it was his turn to facilitate their escape. He'd make sure they reached the small cave he'd spotted earlier.

"I think we should make our move," he said. "The miners won't risk returning with the helicopter flying around. They'll be afraid of the pilot reporting unauthorized motorized vehicles in the area."

Kate nodded. "Agreed."

"First, let's take off our ponchos."

Serene frowned. "We'll get soaked."

"We're already soaked," Brie said.

Rand sat up gradually, keeping watch for any movement. "The ponchos are easy to see from a distance." He stripped off his plastic poncho and stuffed it inside his jacket.

Kate did the same. Then they helped the girls with

their ponchos. It was an arduous ordeal after lying for so long on the cold, wet ground. Rand's stiff muscles ached. And he'd have no relief.

He reminded himself he'd been through considerably worse after the accident. This was nothing in comparison. He'd manage his pain for all their sakes. If not, Kate and the girls might not survive.

The cave was farther away than Rand had first estimated. It took them over an hour of bone-crunching, muscle-cramping climbing, constantly on the lookout for the miners, to reach the small hole in the side of the mountain. When they did, they collapsed on the ledge with exhaustion.

After catching their breath, Rand urged them inside. They'd been traveling in the open long enough, and he was anxious for them to be hidden from view. Only then could he relax.

The space was no bigger than five-by-five feet. They were forced to crouch, the ceiling too low for them to stand. The rocky floor and walls weren't designed for comfort and dug into their aching bodies when they sat. But they were safe and shielded from the rain. For now.

"I'm thirsty," Brie repeated for about the tenth time.

With the heavy downpour, it was hard to imagine wanting something to drink. Rand reached just outside the shelter with his cupped hands, which he then brought to his lips.

Serene stared at him in shock. "You expect us to drink rain?"

He gathered enough for another few sips. "It's not awful."

"And full of germs that'll make us sick."

"Actually," Kate said, moving to the opening next

to Rand, "rainwater directly from the sky isn't that bad for you. It's only when water sits in a barrel or a bucket and stagnates that you can get sick."

Where had she learned that? Rand wondered. And then felt terrible that she'd *had* to learn. He didn't like imagining Kate being in such dire straits she had no access to even tap water.

"I'll try," Brie said when Rand had returned to his spot against the shelter wall.

Serene huffed but then joined her foster sister.

Kate settled next to Rand, and the two of them watched the girls drink. For a few seconds, Serene and Brie made light of the situation, splashing and teasing each other. When they finished, they sat near the cave entrance, looking out and chatting softly. They were clearly close, and watching them gave Rand hope.

He leaned toward Kate and whispered, "That Serene is something else."

"She's had a hard go of it, for sure. I feel sorry for her."

"Me, too." Now that they were relatively safe, exhaustion overcame him, and he leaned his head against the wall, not even caring about the sharp rocks digging into his scalp.

"How are your legs?" Kate asked.

"I wouldn't turn down a couple of ibuprofens if you had any." What he'd give for a soak in Ansel's hot tub along with the pills.

"Wish I did." Kate opened her fanny pack and dug around the contents. She still had the pocketknife and empty canister of pepper spray, without which they might not have gotten away.

"You did good back there," he said. "That took courage and quick thinking."

"You're the one who did good. I wasn't expecting you to tackle the guy. You play football in high school as well as rodeoing?"

"A little. I was better at bronc and bull riding."

"You were great at bronc and bull riding. I saw you compete a few times. Well, more than a few times. Rodeo was my life back then."

"I saw you compete, too," he admitted. "I knew your sister better."

"Everyone knew my sister. Comes with being a junior rodeo queen."

Kate made the comment with neither jealousy nor pride, which piqued Rand's curiosity. Were they close? Her sister had definitely been more popular than Kate and a better competitor.

How much did that have to do with her decision to participate in the prank? During the trial, she'd claimed that she'd wanted to impress the boy who'd been Rand's rival and the ringleader. It couldn't have been easy for her, living in the shadow of her much more accomplished sister.

"You see her often?" he asked. "Your sister."

"No." Kate removed two power bars from her fanny pack. "Not for years. My parents, either."

That took Rand aback. "You're kidding?"

"I wish I was. They're ashamed of me."

He wanted to say he didn't understand how they could feel like that. Then he remembered his hatred for Kate after the accident. For the first time, he suffered a stab of guilt. He'd been hard on her. Harder than necessary.

"Their choice," she continued, her voice cracking. "Not mine."

"That's a shame."

She tossed Brie and Serene one of the power bars. "Here, girls."

"Only one?" Serene asked.

"That's all I brought. You'll have to share."

"Are there any, like, berries we can pick or something?"

"None safe to eat," Rand said.

The girls polished off the power bar and went back to chatting.

Kate opened the remaining power bar and broke it in half, giving one piece to Rand.

He thought about refusing but reconsidered. Kate wouldn't eat if he didn't.

"My brother and I are in contact," she continued, "if you call the occasional email contact. He keeps me updated on the family and vice versa, I guess. I've told him more than once if Mom and Dad and my sister ever change their minds, I would love to hear from them. So far, they haven't taken me up on the offer."

"They're missing out by not knowing you, Kate."

She turned and met his gaze. "That's not something I ever expected you to say."

He didn't look away, captivated by her earnest expression and compelling hazel eyes. "I've been angry. I won't lie."

"You've had every right."

"I blamed you more than I should have. You were just a pawn used by those boys. I was too stubborn to see that before. And I needed somewhere to vent my rage."

She nodded.

"I'm truly sorry about what happened to you in prison. I feel responsible."

"Don't." She placed her hand on his arm. "That's entirely on me."

Until very recently, Rand would have recoiled from her touch. Now he took the gesture as it was intended—extending an olive branch.

He amazed himself with his next words and the way they naturally sprang from his mouth. "Maybe when we get home, we can start over."

"Start over how?" she asked, uncertainty clouding her expression.

"I'm not sure exactly."

"Do you honestly think we're capable of being friends?"

He could see she was worried about getting hurt and, possibly, hurting him again. "I think we're capable of being friendly coworkers. It's a start."

She hesitated before admitting, "I'd like that."

"Me, too."

They hadn't been this close, physically or emotionally, since the day of the accident when he'd kissed her cheek moments before his event and while his rival was sabotaging the saddle on his bronc. The sense of closeness he felt with Kate remained even after she withdrew her hand from his.

Biting into her power bar, she encouraged him to do the same. By then, Serene and Brie had moved away from the opening and were sitting across from them, Brie's head resting on Serene's shoulder.

Rand unbuttoned his jacket. The balled-up rain poncho fell out onto his lap. "Let's everyone take off our coats. See if we can't dry them and ourselves off a little." He doubted there was much chance of that, what with the damp air inside the shelter and no fire. Their shirts, however, might dry from body heat, which wouldn't happen if they continued to wear their wet jackets.

The girls laid out their jackets and ponchos on the shelter floor. Kate hung hers from protruding rocks on the wall. Rand did the same.

"What next?" Serene asked.

Rand noticed her tone was more serious and less snide. "We rest for a while. As long as we don't hear any engines or see the ATVs, we head out late afternoon."

"And go where?"

"I think we continue to stay high and travel parallel to the trail. It traverses the mountains and will eventually lead us out of the Superstitions."

"That won't be easy," Kate said. "The terrain is steeper on this side."

She didn't ask, but he heard the question. Was he physically capable? "We don't have much choice."

"What about the lightning?"

"As of right now, there isn't any. If it starts again, we'll find another shelter."

She didn't look reassured. Neither did the girls.

"The miners are less likely to come searching for us at night," he said.

"Or, more likely," Kate countered. "The cover of darkness hides them as much as us."

She had a valid argument. Meeting her worried gaze, Rand couldn't guarantee his plan was the absolute right course of action. He knew only that they were choosing the lesser of two evils—and that they would be facing the same tough choice every step of the way home.

Chapter Eight

They prepared to leave the shelter later that afternoon. Kate had tried to nap and encouraged the others to do the same. No one had. They were too afraid of the miners reappearing. And the stony shelter floor didn't lend itself to comfort.

Instead, they'd talked quietly, prayed and rested. Kate stayed beside Rand the entire time, his proximity bringing her a modicum of peace. While he hadn't specifically said the words, she felt from their earlier conversation that he'd forgiven her, or was at least considering the possibility.

Perhaps they'd reached an understanding. He'd said he wanted them to start over, and Kate's spirits lifted at the prospect. It was one more reason for them to get safely home.

The rain continued to fall in a light drizzle. That could change to a deluge at any moment, however.

"My jacket's still damp," Serene said, fingering the hem.

"Can't be helped." Kate adjusted her shirt collar. The fabric had begun to itch. "At least our ponchos are dry.

We can wear them under our jackets. They'll keep us warm and provide a barrier between our clothes and damp outerwear."

"We'll also be less visible," Rand added.

Kate grimaced while donning her damp jacket. She wasn't the only one.

Rand insisted on exiting the shelter first. Crouching in front of the opening, he paused to assess their situation.

"See anything?" Kate asked, peering over his shoulder.

"No. But that means nothing. The miners could be hiding anywhere." He glanced toward the neighboring mountain as if expecting them to come roaring over the top.

"Let's pray that they're back at their camp, packing and destroying the evidence."

Kate remembered the dead hiker and silently asked God to watch over his companion, wherever she was, and to bring his family comfort when they learned what had happened to him.

"Look there," Rand said. "In the bottom of the ravine."

"What is it?" She squinted, trying to discern shapes in the gray light.

"Horses."

Her pulse drummed as she frantically tried to locate the animals. "I don't see them."

"Near the cluster of trees."

The girls pushed up alongside Kate.

"Our horses are back." Serene jostled Kate's arm. "We have to catch them."

"Not our horses," Rand said and sat back on his heels. "These are wild."

Kate finally spotted the small herd threading in and out between the trees. "How can you tell?"

"There're more than four. Six or seven, by my count. And there's a black-and-white paint in the bunch. None of our four is a paint. Plus, they don't have saddles."

Kate at last glimpsed the lead horse and a yearling. Sadly, she had to agree with Rand. These weren't Still Water Ranch horses.

"I wish we could ride them," Brie lamented.

"Even if we had a rope or some means of capturing them," Rand said, "they haven't had much human contact, if any."

Kate thought, from a distance, this ragtag lot appeared docile.

"Didn't some of the wild horses in these parts originally come from ranches?"

"A few. They either escaped or ran off or were set free."

"Who would set a horse free?" Serene asked.

"It can happen. Last year, one of the ranches near Still Water had a barn fire. The owner freed the horses in order to save them from being burned. Afterward, they couldn't find one of them and think it disappeared into the mountains."

"We could always approach them," Kate suggested.

"We can't reach them fast enough. They'll see us coming and scatter."

Serene huffed. "So what, then? We just keep walking? Do you even know which direction to go?"

"I do."

Kate appreciated Rand's patience with Serene. He could have snapped at her. As recently as yesterday, he might have done just that.

"How long will it take us to walk out?" Serene asked.

"We won't be moving as fast as the horses. Two days, tops."

"Two days!"

"Tops," he repeated. "More than likely, people will be searching for us by the morning, assuming the worst of the storm is behind us. I'm hoping we run into them."

Kate shivered. If the miners didn't find them first.

"Let's head out." Rand stood, his movements awkward and stiff.

He set out, and the rest of them followed in the same order as before—the girls in between Rand and Kate. The going was every bit as grueling, the mountain's steep incline tiring their legs. Keeping low to the ground strained their backs and shoulders. They had to stop and rest every twenty to thirty minutes.

Kate gave the girls credit. There were no complaints. Then again, perhaps they were too weary to complain.

Just as the last vestiges of dusk were fading into night, Kate spotted a movement ahead, nearer to the trail. At first, she thought her eyes were deceiving her and wiped away the rain with the back of her hand. A second look confirmed it. Someone was there!

"Rand! Look. About three o'clock. There's something or someone moving through the brush."

They all stopped and, it seemed, collectively held their breaths. Rand stared intently.

"See him? Or it?" She couldn't tell if the dark shape was a person or an animal. Her heart drummed faster and faster. There were no bears in these mountains. A deer perhaps? A mountain lion?

"Not him," Rand said. "Her. I'm pretty sure it's the woman hiker."

"What! Really? You can tell?"

"See the ball cap and backpack?"

Kate didn't see, but she trusted him.

"She must have gotten away from the miners."

"Thank God. Should we holler at her?" The woman wasn't that far away. They could reach her quickly and then help each other get home.

"She's spotted us," Rand said and raised his arm in the air.

And just like that, the woman slipped away into the darkness. A moment later, it was as if she'd never been there.

"She's afraid of us," Kate said.

"I'd be afraid, too, if someone had killed my companion."

"I'm glad she's gone." Serene hugged her waist and frowned. "I know the guy's dead and all, but she was weird."

"Serene, don't say that," Brie admonished, her eyes filled with fright. "God won't like it. He might punish us."

"That's ridiculous." But Serene glanced warily at the sky.

Brie's remark struck a chord with Kate. At one time, when she'd first started attending prison worship services, she'd had similar thoughts—that she was being punished for her role in Rand's accident. Then she learned differently. She'd come to believe she was being tested and failed not once but often.

"God isn't like that." She squeezed the girl's shoulder. "He doesn't punish people for thinking ill of someone."

"Mr. Laurent's been telling us stories from the Bible," Brie countered. "About the vengeance of God."

How could Kate explain a complicated concept to a twelve-year-old who had only read the Bible for the first time in the past few days?

"Mr. Laurent's been telling you those stories so that you and all of us might see a little of ourselves in the people and strive to become better. Kinder. More understanding. More tolerant."

She caught Rand watching her. He nodded slightly.

"Serene." Kate turned to the other girl. "When I was in prison, I met a lot of inmates who were different than me. And that made me uncomfortable. Even scared. I agree that we should keep our distance from dangerous people, but appearances can be deceiving. That woman hiker is probably terrified right now. I'm thinking, like us, she and the man accidentally stumbled on the illegal mining operation, and only she got away. Even if she is weird, we should help her if we can."

Serene started to whimper softly. "I want to go home. I don't want to be here."

"I know, sweetie. We all want that." She found Rand's glance again. "And we'll find a way."

"We will," he agreed.

A few hours later, they took cover beneath a rocky overhang. Cold, hungry and spent, they could go no farther without a rest. The rain had stopped an hour earlier, and there'd been no sign of the miners. Their optimism rose.

"My guess is it's around nine or ten," Rand said as he sat next to Kate. "I think we should spend the remainder of the night here and try to get some sleep. If the coast is clear come morning, we'll continue and hopefully run into someone who can help us."

"I'm hungry," Brie said.

"I'm cold," Serene added. She'd been quiet since the discussion about God's vengeance.

"Let's sit closer together." Kate pulled Brie to her, and Serene snuggled against Brie.

Though only about sixty-five degrees out, being damp and miserable made them feel much colder. One good thing about the weather, if not for the overcast skies they'd be battling heatstroke. Temperatures reached one hundred degrees and higher this time of year. If it were winter, they'd be suffering from hypothermia.

Eventually, everyone quieted, and the hours dragged by. Sleep didn't come easy for Kate and Rand. The chilly and rocky ground, combined with their cramped sitting positions, and the constant fear they'd be discovered, kept them wide awake for most of the night. The girls dozed in fits and starts. Kate nodded off once, only to awaken with a jolt and find herself slumped against Rand.

"Sorry about that," she whispered and straightened. "You should have woken me."

"I didn't mind," he said.

Kate refused to read anything more into his statement than that: he didn't mind. When people were frightened, being close to someone, anyone, provided comfort. Once, during a riot in the prison cafeteria, she'd crouched beneath a table and held the hand of a woman who was two hundred and fifty pounds of solid muscle, with a face covered in scars and three missing teeth. Until then, Kate had avoided her at all costs.

"Okay." She moved, putting a few inches between her and Rand.

He reached for her hand and folded it inside his. "I didn't mind," he repeated, squeezing her fingers.

She squeezed back but kept her face averted, too

afraid if she looked at him, he'd see emotions stirring in her she wasn't ready to reveal.

They stayed like that for several minutes until the girls roused.

"What time is it?" Serene asked drowsily.

Rand leaned forward and peered outside. "Just after dawn, judging by the sky."

"We should get started." Kate shifted and stretched her stiff legs. Once they were out from beneath the overhang, she examined the sky. "It looks like we're in for more rain."

"Unfortunately, I think you're right," Rand said. "Soon, by the looks of it. We need to make tracks and put as much distance as possible between us and the miners while we can."

Without falling rain, finding drinkable water presented a problem. Kate located a shallow pool in the concave top of a boulder. They took turns scooping out handfuls.

"Ew. It tastes gross." Serene made a face.

"Are you sure it's safe to drink?" Brie asked, cautiously studying the pool.

"I doubt the water's sat long enough to stagnate." Kate took several swallows, attempting to encourage the girls. It did have an earthy flavor.

Once they'd satisfied their thirst, they headed out, following the same course as the day before—parallel to the south-easterly trail and thirty yards higher. The going continued to be hard and their progress slow. In addition to exhaustion, cold and aching muscles, hunger weakened them. The longer they went without seeing a search party or encountering a hiker, the lower their spirits sank.

Kate kept a constant lookout for trouble and tried not

to think about the giant hollow hole in her middle. If not for the weather and their constant fear of the miners, they'd have likely encountered a search party by now or a friendly hiker.

As if her thoughts had conjured her worst fear, she suddenly heard the sound of a distant engine. Rand ground to a halt and extended his arm to the side to stop her and the girls.

Not again! Kate's heart cried out as an all too familiar current of fear raced through her.

"Wait here while I take a look," Rand told Kate.

Ignoring his shooting pain and the pouring rain, he crouched low and crab-walked to a vantage point higher on the mountain. Peering between the branches of a prickly pear cactus, he surveyed the valley below, seeking the source of the engine sound.

And then he saw it! About a quarter mile away, in the bottom of the ravine, an ATV darted in and out of the trees. Every nerve in his body went on high alert.

"Are the miners back?"

He turned to see Kate climbing up the mountainside and let out a groan of frustration. "I told you to wait."

She crawled toward him. "Are they?"

"There's only one ATV, as far as I can tell, and I don't think it's a miner. The guy's coming from the direction of the maintenance road and wearing a cowboy hat instead of a helmet." He looked again. "The ATV's red and white, not black, and a heavy-duty model. The miners are driving smaller and more streamlined ATVs."

"He could be their scout. Or someone who transports their supplies."

"Only one way to find out." Rand checked the gun stuffed into his waistband.

"What are you doing?" Kate asked in alarm.

"Introducing myself."

"He could hurt you."

"I don't believe he's one of the miners." Rand put a hand on her shoulder. "But just in case I'm wrong, you stay hidden."

"We can't lose you." Her tone and gaze were both filled with panic. "I can't lose you."

"Kate," he said her name, hearing a softness in his voice that hadn't been there before. Not when it came to her. "We need help, and this guy may have a phone. I have to take the chance."

"He's riding an ATV. Those are illegal in the mountains. And it's raining. He can't be up to any good."

"People who aren't criminals break minor laws all the time. He's probably thinking no one's out today, and he won't get caught."

"It's too risky."

Rand studied the man on the ATV as he drew nearer. He didn't appear dangerous. And if he had a phone or a radio, they'd be home in a matter of hours rather than a day or two.

"I need to hurry. If I don't, he'll be gone and may not return."

"Be careful. Please." Kate's fingers squeezed his arm. "Come back to me."

"I will." He suspected there was a more personal meaning to her request and his response but exploring it would have to wait. "Go back to the girls. They shouldn't be alone."

She released him. "God be with you."

"If anything happens, don't come after me. You find a place for you and the girls to hide and get away at night. Just like we were planning."

"Rand, no!"

"You have to, Kate. I need to know you'll be safe."

How often would they have this same conversation? When would the danger end?

She nodded, tears springing to her eyes.

He left, resisting the urge to pull her into his arms.

Rocks crunched beneath his boots as he made his way down the mountainside as fast as his weakened legs could carry him. His gaze never left the man on the ATV drawing nearer and nearer.

When Rand reached the ravine's edge, he raised his arms and waved wildly. The man didn't notice him. Rand waved again and hollered. "Hey! Stop!"

The man was almost directly beneath him, still zig-zagging in and out of the trees. Rand panicked: afraid the man would pass right by without ever seeing him.

Cupping his hands around his mouth, he yelled at the top of his lungs, "Hello! Up here."

Thankfully, the man raised his head. Spotting Rand above the treetops, he waved in return and slowed the ATV to a stop, letting the engine idle.

His relief was short-lived. The man's actions too closely mimicked those of the miner outside their camp. *Please, Lord, let him be a Good Samaritan.*

"Hang on, buddy." Rand gathered his courage and climbed down the ravine. In his haste, he slipped and fell twice, grabbing branches to right himself. By the time he reached the bottom, his palms were scraped and bleeding.

The man smiled as Rand approached. "What in blue blazes are you doing out here alone and on foot?"

Rand remained cautious, his hand hovering near the gun concealed beneath his jacket. The man's pleasant greeting could be a ruse. "Well, that's an interesting story."

"I'm all ears."

The man appeared in his early to mid-sixties. Small and wiry, his grizzled features might have been carved by an artist. He wore boots and jeans, a worn canvas coat, along with the cowboy hat Rand had spotted earlier. He didn't resemble the miners, though he could be aiding them, as Kate had suggested.

Then again, if he was, he'd likely be carrying a weapon and Rand would be at this moment lying on the ground and drawing his last breath.

Still, he opted for an edited version of the truth. Better to err on the side of caution until he knew if this man was trustworthy. Their lives could be at stake. "We were on a trail ride. I rode ahead and got off my horse for a bit. Made the mistake of not tying him securely. Then the storm hit and scared him. He bolted, and I wasn't fast enough."

"I've had that happen before." The man laughed good-naturedly, cut the ATV's engine and climbed off.

"Anyway," Rand continued, trying to appear non-threatening, "I wound up separated from my friends. Dropped and shattered my phone. By then, it was raining buckets. I didn't much care for the idea of traveling these mountains with all that lightning, so I spent the night in a cave."

"No fooling. That must have been miserable."

Rand thought about sitting next to Kate and their conversation. "Could've been worse."

"I'm surprised your friends didn't come after you."

"That was my fault. I called before my phone busted and told them to go ahead without me. That I wasn't far behind."

"Good thing you ran into me."

Was it? Rand needed to be sure. "What brings you out in this weather?"

"I work for the Double R Cattle Ranch over yonder." He tipped his head toward the south.

"I've heard of them. I'm the manager at Still Water."

"Well, fancy that. We're practically neighbors."

In truth, the two ranches were fifteen miles apart. But Rand didn't split hairs.

"We lost some cattle during the storm last night," he continued. "Thunder scared them, like your horse, I reckon, and they broke through the pasture fence. A hundred head. Been rounding them up since daybreak. I'm looking for stragglers. About a dozen still missing."

Rand was starting to feel better about the situation. The man's story sounded plausible.

"Do you have a phone on you?" he asked.

"I do. It ain't been working for the last hour. No bars. But you're welcome to try."

He fished a battered flip phone out of his coat and handed it to Rand, who wasted no time attempting to reach the ranch. Sadly, he couldn't get a signal, either.

"Can you do me a favor?" He returned the phone. "Would you call Still Water Ranch as soon as you get somewhere with bars, let them know you talked to me and give them my location?"

"I can do you one better than that." The man grinned.

"I'll drive you to the trailhead. Someone can meet you there. We might even run across your horse on the way."

Rand's excitement soared, only to crash abruptly. He couldn't leave Kate and the girls behind. He *wouldn't* leave them. Not for anything.

"I really appreciate the offer, pal, but I'm going to have to pass."

"Are you joking?" The man drew back, his expression incredulous.

Rand hesitated, weighing his options. Finally, he admitted, "I'm not alone."

"No?" The man's brows rose and then drew together in a suspicious V. "Is something funny going on here?"

"Not what you think." Rand made another snap decision. Turning, he hollered up the ravine, "Kate, girls. It's okay. You can come down." When they didn't immediately respond, he hollered again. "It's safe. I promise."

Chapter Nine

After twice more calling to Kate with no response, Rand began to worry. He shouldn't have left them behind. If something happened, he wouldn't forgive himself.

"You think you should go after them?" the man asked, still frowning. He must think Rand was lying, since Kate and the girls hadn't appeared.

Then it hit him. She was afraid a miner had captured him and wanted her and the girls, too. He had to say something that would convince her Rand spoke the truth and not lies he'd been forced to say at gunpoint.

"He's from the Double R Cattle Ranch and searching for stragglers. God has sent him to help us."

Another few seconds passed before she hollered "Okay."

Rand tracked her and the girls' progress down the ravine. When they emerged from between the trees, they approached slowly and wore guarded expressions.

"Well, paint me green and call me a pickle," the man said, taking them in. "Would you look at that."

"Kate also works at Still Water," Rand said. "And the girls are part of our Youth Wrangler Camp."

"I've heard of that." The man smiled in greeting. "Howdy there. Name's Dermot Ebersol. That's quite a mouthful, so most folks call me Eb."

Kate nodded and murmured, "Nice to meet you."

The girls stared wordlessly. Rand clearly hadn't done enough to ease their fears. He needed to change that.

"Eb's going to call the ranch and report our location as soon as he gets to a place where his phone works. Let them know we're making our way to the trailhead."

"I sure will." Eb patted his pocket. "Rand plugged in the ranch number while we were waiting on you."

"What if…" Kate hesitated. Her gaze traveled from Eb to Rand. "What if Eb took the girls with him? They could both fit on the back of the ATV."

"That's not a bad idea," Rand agreed. Serene and Brie should get away while they had the chance in case the illegal miners returned.

"No way!" Serene blurted and fired a suspicious glare at Eb. "We don't know this dude."

"I don't want to leave, either," Brie said. "He could be a creep."

"I'm not." Eb chuckled. "But she has a point. The trailhead's no more than a two or three-hour drive from here. Won't be long before someone's coming after you."

Rand considered how much, if anything, to tell the older man. He decided the girls' safety was too important.

"The thing is, Eb," he started only to pause. "There're some illegal miners in the area. Armed and dangerous miners."

Eb's bushy silver brows rose. "You don't say?"

"We inadvertently stumbled onto their campsite, and they aren't happy with us. Some hikers did, too. One of them didn't make it out alive. We've been evading them ever since."

"That's incredible." He stared at them in shock. "It's a wonder the lot of you are all right."

Rand continued. "You understand why we need you to get Serene and Brie to safety."

"Of course. I just wish I could take all of you with me."

"They could shoot at you."

"I know this area well. I'll stay out of sight." Eb scratched the back of his neck. "How in the world do you reckon those miners carried on without getting caught?"

"That'll be for the authorities to figure out when we notify them." Rand looked to the girls. "You need to hurry."

"I don't want to go," Serene repeated.

Eb smiled warmly, his entire countenance changing. "Hey, youngins. I know how you feel. It's scary, the idea of riding off with an old geezer you just met. I got me a couple of granddaughters about your age, and their parents have taught them to never speak to strangers. I'm sure your parents told you the same thing. But you can trust me. I promise. And if it'll make you feel better, I'll let one of you carry my phone. And call the ranch when we get a signal."

The idea appealed to Rand. Not so much Serene and Brie. They looked to Kate for reassurance. She drew them close to her for a hug.

"You need to go with Eb," she said.

"Will you and Rand be okay?" Brie asked in a worried voice.

"Yes." Kate's gaze sought his. "We'll be fine."

Brie sobbed softly.

For once, Serene showed compassion. She clasped

her foster sister's hand and said "We can do this" with newly displayed strength and confidence. "Mr. Laurent says that sometimes you just have to trust in the Lord."

The Lord, yes, thought Rand. And an older man by the name of Dermot Ebersol.

Before climbing onto the ATV, the girls hugged Kate as if they might never see her again. Rand noticed Kate slipping Serene her pocketknife. He didn't think the girls would need it, but if having a weapon, albeit a small one, made them feel better, that was fine by him.

"Thanks, Eb." Rand shook the other man's hand. "You're a Godsend."

"Happy to help."

"Sorry I took you away from searching for those stragglers."

"Oh, we'll find them eventually. If not, somebody else will and return them to us."

Rand figured Ed was right. While there were feral horses in the mountains, cattle were different. Most had identifying ear tags, and their owners could be easily tracked down. If the stragglers weren't reported by hikers or horseback riders, a forest ranger patrolling the area would spot them. It was possible an unscrupulous individual might keep the cattle, but stealing was illegal and, if caught, the individual would be arrested.

"Hold on tight," Kate instructed the girls.

Brie sat sandwiched between Eb and Serene, her arms around his waist. Serene had her arms around Brie's middle.

"Don't you fret," Eb said and started the engine. "I'll take good care of these two."

"See you soon." Kate waved as the ATV pulled away.

Both girls stared over their shoulders at her and Rand, their expressions a mixture of anxiety and uncertainty.

Rand and Kate stayed where they were, watching, until the ATV was out of sight behind the trees. Even then, they didn't move, not until the whine of the engine faded to silence.

Rand shielded his eyes from the rain and inspected the sky. No indication of the storm abating. "We should get going."

Kate didn't move.

"They'll be fine."

She sighed. "I know."

He offered her an encouraging smile. "If we hurry, it's possible we'll be home in time for dinner and some of Mrs. Sciacca's beef stew."

"That would be nice." She squared her shoulders and took a determined step forward.

They returned to the high ground above the trail, the climb no less difficult than before. While Rand felt better about not encountering the illegal miners again, they couldn't be too careful and continued to use the brush and cacti for cover.

Near midmorning—or later, the rain and overcast sky interfered with Rand's internal clock—he calculated they'd traveled close to two miles. Though he couldn't be sure of that, either.

"You ready for a rest?" Kate asked. She didn't mention his heavy breathing and pronounced limping.

"In a few minutes. The halfway mark to the trailhead is just up there." No sooner had he spoken than lightning flashed and thunder cracked.

"The storm's worsening. We're going to need to find cover."

So much for resting.

Around the next bend, they walked into a dense expanse of cacti that covered the entire mountainside. Forced to stop, they assessed their next move. Below them lay the ravine, this part of it crowded with mature mesquite trees in full foliage.

"What if we get out of these cacti and travel down there instead?" Kate pointed to the ravine. "The trees would hide us and protect us from the storm."

"If the miners come this way, they'll be using the ravine and run right into us."

"We haven't seen a sign of them in a while."

Was it worth the risk? Rand deliberated. Death by lightning strike or by a miner's bullet?

As if his thoughts had manufactured them, three gunshots fired in quick succession echoed through the valley. He grabbed Kate by the arm and pulled her to the ground alongside him.

"Are you all right?" he growled.

"Yes." Her entire body shook. "Are you?"

A bad feeling came over Rand. "I don't think they were shooting at us."

"Who then?"

The sudden look of fear in her eyes said she'd figured it out. "The girls. And Eb. We need to find them." She started to rise.

He restrained her. "Not until we know it's safe."

"What if they're in trouble?"

"The miners could have been shooting at someone else."

"Like us?"

He shrugged. "Eb was out here riding around. Maybe there are others."

"I hate the idea of anyone being shot at."

Rand, too. "The ATVs didn't pass us. Which means they took a different route. If we head out, we could be walking right into a trap."

"I can't just sit here waiting." Kate squeezed her hands into fists.

He gentled his voice. "I know this is hard. But if we're dead or injured, we'll be of no help to anyone."

"Five minutes."

"Kate."

"Five minutes," she repeated. "And then I'm going in search of the girls and Eb with or without you."

She was serious. When he could no longer hold her back, they proceeded, keeping behind the cover of brush as they headed down the mountainside into the ravine and the safety of the trees. Rand let out a long exhale, only to tense. The miners could appear around the next bend at any moment. The absence of additional gunshots or the sounds of an engine didn't ease his worries.

They'd traveled twenty minutes over increasingly wet ground when a thin cry pierced the air.

Kate gasped. "Did you hear that?"

Rand tried to determine the direction the cry had come from. "I'd say they're a few hundred yards ahead."

Kate turned toward him, her expression radiating alarm. "Isn't that the way Eb and the girls went?"

"Yes, but—"

The cry came again, this time louder. Rand's heart pounded.

Kate grabbed his arm and started to run, pulling him along. "That's Brie! I recognize her voice."

Kate didn't stop to think. Neither did she worry about the risks. The girls were in trouble. How had that happened? A short time ago, they'd been heading off to safety on the back of Eb's ATV.

She tripped, her ankle twisting. That didn't deter her. Neither did Rand, who cautioned her to slow down and let him go first.

"Brie, Serene. Where are you?"

"Here," came Brie's faint reply. "Help us."

"She's on the other side of that bend," Rand said.

In this part of the mountains, trees and brush grew more abundantly. As a result, the ground wasn't as loose, the vegetation's root systems providing support— and also more obstacles.

Kate tripped and let out a loud "Oomph."

Rand grabbed her arm before she face-planted. "You okay?"

"We have to hurry."

Though only a few minutes had passed since they'd first heard Brie, it felt like an hour. Kate's legs trembled from the exertion. Rand's must be ten times worse.

"Hold on!" she hollered. "We're almost there."

She and Rand forged ahead through the mesquite trees, heedless of the prickly branches. The once shallow stream traversing the ravine had swelled to a fast-flowing creek three feet deep in the middle.

Why hadn't they thought about the ravine filling with runoff from the mountains? Stupid, stupid, stupid!

They avoided the water, which could easily drag them under, and pushed onward. By now, Kate's lungs burned. She frantically searched among the trees for any sign of the girls and Eb and prayed for their safety.

When Rand cut ahead of her, she caught sight of his face and gasped. "You're hurt."

"It's nothing."

The oozing gashes crisscrossing his cheek didn't look like nothing. She'd tend them later. After they found the girls and Eb.

"There they are," Rand said with urgency.

Kate spied Brie between the trees. She appeared okay. But what about Serene and Eb?

The trees parted and gave way to a clearing. Kate cried out at the sight of the overturned ATV lying on the side of the creek a foot from the water. Brie stood near it. There was no sign of Serene and Eb.

Rand covered the remaining distance separating them in a few strides, Kate right behind him. Rain pelted their faces. The trees, while annoying, had shielded them from the worst of the storm.

"Kate!" Brie ran toward them, her expression changing from wild with fear to relief. "We crashed. The guy's hurt."

"Where is he?" Rand demanded.

"Here," came Eb's disembodied voice. "I'm stuck beneath the ATV."

"I'm here, too," Serene said. "I'm okay."

Oh, dear Lord. Kate hugged Brie to her, relieved beyond belief. Eb was injured, but not shot. "What about you? Were you injured?"

Brie shook her head.

Kate closed her eyes before releasing the girl and skirting the ATV. Nothing prepared her for the sight of Eb pinned beneath the vehicle or Serene sitting on the ground beside him, tenderly holding his hand.

"How bad are you hurt?" Kate asked.

Eb grunted. "I'll live. As long as you can get this contraption off me. I'd do it myself, but I can't get twisted around enough."

"You stay put." Rand studied the ATV.

"We heard gunshots," Serene explained. "Eb started speeding, and that's why we crashed."

"Guess those miners you warned me about showed up." Eb shifted and winced. The weight of the ATV lying across his thighs was taking a toll on him. His normally ruddy cheeks were pale and drawn.

"I'm sorry, buddy," Rand said.

"Hey, not your fault. I stuck to the trees. They must've caught sight of us. When the shots started, I put the pedal to the metal. Figured I could lose them in the ravine, or they'd give up. Everything was fine until that curve came out of nowhere. I lost control, and we took a spill."

"It appears you did lose them."

Eb grunted. "That's good."

Serene stood and stepped away, giving Rand room. She didn't take her eyes off Eb, even when Brie scurried around to join her.

Seeing them together, Kate suppressed a sob. How could she have suggested Eb take the girls when the illegal miners were still roaming the mountains? If anything had happened to them, Kate would have never forgiven herself.

Eb attempted to sit up. The effort proved too much for him, and he slumped back down. "Son of a gun."

"Hold on a minute." Rand knelt beside Eb and checked the older man's lower legs. Kate assumed Rand was feeling for a pulse, ensuring that Eb hadn't lost blood flow. Where had he learned to do that?

"Can we lift the ATV off him?" she asked. She was no expert, but the thing was huge and had to weigh over three hundred pounds.

"I think so." Rand's glance cut to Kate. It said, *We*

need to lift it off before he suffers irreparable damage to his legs. "You ready for that?" He gave Eb's shoulder a squeeze.

"More than ready."

"Might hurt a bit when your circulation kicks in. And you could have broken something."

"We'll just have to see." Eb coughed and coughed, covering his mouth with his forearm until the fit passed.

"All right, pal," Rand said. "Let's get you out from under this ATV."

"How do we do that?" Kate asked.

"We lift it."

She wasn't sure if she had any strength left, but she would find it somehow.

"You, Serene and Brie, come over to this side." Rand motioned. "Kate, to my left. Girls, to my right. Grab hold of the side of the ATV and, when I say go, lift as high as you can. I'll pull Eb out from underneath."

The girls stared at him with dubious expressions. Kate related.

"You can do it." Rand nodded confidently. "Eb, grit your teeth."

"Don't you worry about me," the older man said. "Just get me clear of this thing."

They all needed a few minutes to get in position. Kate gripped the side of the ATV, the metal cool on her palms, and readied herself.

"Okay?" Rand asked. His question was met by a round of assents. "Go."

The girls and Kate lifted the ATV with all their might, managing to raise it nearly a foot off the ground. Rand hooked his hands beneath Eb's arms and dragged the older man forward, his backside scraping across the damp rocks. Eb moaned but resisted crying out. Kate imagined it felt like a thousand needles piercing his poor legs as blood resumed flowing.

Once he was clear of harm's way, Rand stopped pulling and blew out a long breath as he straightened. Kate and the girls dropped the ATV, which creaked and rattled when it landed.

"Eb, are you all right?" Rand asked.

"Better now."

With his help, the older man sat up.

He examined Eb's legs, gently pressing here and there. "Does anything hurt?"

Eb let out a howl. "That does."

"Hurt like a broken leg?"

He chuckled weakly. "To be honest, I can't tell. Maybe if I stand."

Rand took one of Eb's arms, and Kate the other. Together, they hoisted him to his feet. He wobbled but didn't fall.

"You're favoring your left leg," Kate observed.

"Am I?"

He appeared disoriented. Kate wondered if he was in shock.

"Can you put any weight on it?" Rand asked.

Eb tried. "Not much. Give me a little time, though. I can walk off the pain."

Unlikely, thought Kate.

"Ew!" Serene made a face. "Is that blood?"

"Where?" Kate automatically examined herself.

"Eb's leg."

A dark spot the size of a baseball stained his pants right above the knee and was spreading fast. Something sharp on the ATV must have cut his leg. No wonder he couldn't put any weight on it.

"We'd better have a look at that." Kate sat him on the ATV's rear tire and rolled up his pant leg. A nasty wound ran down the side of his thigh. The weight of the heavy ATV had staunched the bleeding until Eb was pulled free and stood. Now the wound oozed bright red blood. "I don't suppose you're carrying a first aid kit on that ATV?"

Eb shook his head. "Been meaning to replace the old one. Now I wish I'd gotten around to it."

She glanced up at Rand. "We need to bind his leg."

"Will this work?" He produced a crumpled bandana from his jeans pocket and passed it to her.

Kate hesitated. "Is it clean?"

"It's the best we've got. Better than him bleeding all over the place."

Beggars couldn't be choosers, she supposed, so she tied the bandana around Eb's shin and fastened a tight knot. Blood instantly soaked the thin material.

"We're going to need more."

Tugging off her boot, she removed her stretchy sock and used it as a tourniquet, applying it just below the knee. Eb volunteered his own bandana. Not great, but it would have to do. Finishing, she straightened and put on her boot. Her skin stuck to the wet leather interior and would be rubbed raw within the first mile of walking.

While she'd been busy with the tourniquet, Rand tried Eb's phone again. Reception remained nonexistent.

"Not sure I can drive with this bum leg," Eb said.

"Don't suppose you can." Rand returned his phone and fallen cowboy hat.

No one mentioned the obvious: Who would drive the ATV and who would be the passengers?

Eb did, however, voice the other important question. "You think it's safe to ride out? I'm in no mood for getting shot at again."

"I agree," Rand said, releasing a long breath. "We should wait."

"For how long?" Eb asked.

"A few hours. Maybe longer. The miners returned once. They could again."

After a rest, perhaps they could decide who stayed and who went.

"I'm hungry." Serene dropped down onto a log.

No one replied. Kate wished she had more power bars. And fresh drinking water. And a first aid kit for Eb. And a working phone.

Frustrated, she kicked at the ground. At the same time, she detected a familiar odor. "Is that gas?"

Rand sniffed the air and frowned. "You're right."

Serene shrieked and jumped back. "The tank's going to explode. I saw it in a movie." She started to run, dragging Brie along with her. "We need to get outta here."

Kate turned to Rand. "Is that true?"

"I don't know. But why take the chance? And I'm sure not driving it with a gas leak."

He and Kate half carried Eb. Beside them, the creek raged. Ahead, the girls stumbled in their haste.

"Where are we going?" Kate asked.

"We stay in the ravine for the time being," Rand said. "Then we'll decide."

"The creek's rising. All but the largest boulders are underwater, and it's already reached the trees."

"We can't leave the ravine. Not yet. Not with the

miners nearby. One good thing about the water—they won't be driving this way."

Despair clung to Kate. There went their hopes of getting home today. And instead of the four of them trying to escape, there were five. With Eb barely able to walk.

Chapter Ten

It seemed to Rand that everything was conspiring against them. The rain had increased steadily during the last hour. They were hungry. Exhaustion hung like one-ton anchors around their necks. Eb's injured leg continued to seep blood despite Kate's diligent ministrations. The miners could reappear at any moment, guns blazing. And Rand's own legs were about as sturdy as a pair of pipe cleaners.

The disabled ATV had been the worst blow. For a precious few hours, Rand and Kate had believed Eb and the girls would reach safety and send back help. Instead, the five of them were trudging along the rocky edge of the ever-swelling creek and trying not to fall in.

Their clothes were soaked through. Kate limped. Rand suspected she sported a blister or two on her sockless foot. The girls were unusually quiet. Eb tried to remain chipper, but he was clearly in agony.

Rand had to do something before fear and discouragement caused them to give up. He stopped and waited for the others to do the same. "I'm going to climb out.

I think we might be near a primitive maintenance road the forest service uses."

"And if we're not?" Kate asked. She supported Eb by the waist. She and Rand had been taking turns assisting him.

"We keep walking."

"No."

"You have a better idea?"

She let out a tired sigh. "We can't stay in the ravine any longer. The creek's four feet deep, at least, and growing more and more treacherous. If Eb falls in, he can't swim in his condition, and the current will carry him away."

"And what about the miners? Do we ignore them?"

"It'll be dark in a few hours," Kate pressed. "I, for one, do not want to be anywhere near this creek then."

She was right. The ravine would be a death trap in the dark.

"Eb, let's try your phone again," Rand said.

Leaning on Kate, the older man reached into the pocket of his jacket and removed the phone. He flipped it open and grumbled under his breath.

"What's wrong?"

"Water got to it." He closed the phone and shook it.

Something else conspiring against them. When would it end?

Rand had to stop thinking like that and concentrate on them being found by Search and Rescue.

Lord, we are struggling. If one small thing could go in our favor, I'd be most grateful.

"We're all gonna die," Serene wailed and threw her arms around Brie.

Both girls started to cry.

"We're not going to die," Rand insisted. "We're going to make it out of here."

No one chimed in to agree with him. And why would they? The last time they believed they were safe, the miners had shot at Eb and the girls.

Rand was almost certain the miners weren't in the area right now. Otherwise, he'd have heard an engine. But what if they'd taken a different route over the mountains? Or, they could have separated. He hadn't considered that before. It was possible he and the others were at this very moment surrounded.

No. He had to stay focused and stop letting his imagination run wild. Concentrate on the present.

"Wait here while I look around," he said. "I won't be long."

The girls found a ledge to sit on. Eb grunted when Kate lowered him onto a boulder. Rand wondered how hard it would be for the injured man to climb out of the ravine. To be honest, Kate and the girls weren't in much better shape. Neither was he.

Once Rand left the trees, he scaled the ravine wall on his hands and knees. It was a long, grueling process. He realized at some point while they were walking, the rain had quit. God's one small favor. That wouldn't affect the rising creek, however. Runoff was always delayed and could continue flowing down the mountains for several hours, if not days, after rain stopped.

With a final burst of energy, Rand hauled himself over the top of the ravine and onto flat ground. He lay for a minute recovering.

A thrashing behind him caused him to roll sideways and glance back down the ravine. His first thought was, why did he never learn?

"Kate, what are you doing?"

"Isn't that obvious?"

"Go back with the others."

She reached him and flopped down, her breathing shallow and rapid.

"What's wrong?" he asked. "Don't you trust me?"

"It's not that."

"You thought I'd need your help."

"I'm here, Rand. Let's not argue."

He started to speak and then changed his mind. Kate had an incredible stubborn streak. He might as well be talking to his boots.

"Fine." He relented and put a hand on her shoulder. "But head low and do as I say." She may not think she needed his protection, but she was going to get it.

"Do you see the miners?"

"No. I'm debating climbing to a higher vantage point."

"That could be dangerous."

"I'll be careful."

He surveyed the area, attempting to gain his bearings. As he'd hoped, they were close to the maintenance road. Straight ahead a quarter of a mile, it was identifiable by a prominent marker post. Weaver's Needle stood tall to the northwest, its red tones muted by the rain.

To the east, a small valley lay between this rise and the next one. Twenty miles to the south, Rand spotted a cluster of square white, tan and black dots. Buildings of some kind.

The irony wasn't lost on him. They could see civilization. But dangerous criminals were in the vicinity and intent on harming them. And unless the storm abated soon, they'd fall victim to the elements.

"Rand. Over there!"

He glanced in the direction Kate indicated and saw the herd of wild horses from before. Soaking wet, they moved slowly through the valley, heads and tails hanging low. Strange that they were traveling in the same direction as Rand and the others and not holed up somewhere beneath the trees, waiting out the storm.

He guessed they must be hungry or were evading a predator. Was that yet another danger to avoid?

"We should try to approach them," Kate said.

"They're feral."

"Maybe, but you said yourself, they could be former ranch horses."

"Even if they were once tame, they've been living in these mountains for who knows how long. They'll be leery of us and run off before we get within fifty feet of them."

"No harm in trying."

"We need to save our energy for the long walk out of here."

"It's just…" She sighed, long and mournfully. "Is this a test? Is God seeing how much we can endure?"

"I don't believe He works like that."

"Me, neither. I'm not sure why I said that."

"We've been through a lot the last two days. Our thoughts are bound to go a little off." Hadn't he recently imagined them surrounded by the miners?

She lifted her face to his, and the despair in her eyes tore at him. He acted without thinking and reached out a hand to cup her cheek. When she leaned into his palm, Rand forgot for a moment where they were and the danger they were in. He also forgot about the anger he'd carried in his heart for years.

Instead, there was just the two of them. He felt like

he was seeing her as someone brand-new and—who would have believed it?—someone he might develop feelings for.

"Rand."

He liked the way she said his name and imagined how it would sound if they were sitting close together in front of the campfire at Still Water Ranch, holding hands and gazing into each other's eyes.

"Don't lose faith," he assured her. "We're going to get home. I promise you."

"Okay."

Gently, he pulled her to him until their foreheads touched. They might have stayed like that for several moments longer, if not for the unmistakable sound of a vehicle horn.

Rand drew back and craned his neck for a better look.

"Is it the miners?" Kate asked, her voice tremulous.

"That didn't sound like an ATV horn."

All at once, a dark SUV appeared on the maintenance road, a quarter mile away. It emerged from the gloom and advanced slowly with the stealth of a wolf tracking prey.

Rand shoved Kate flat and hunkered down beside her.

"Has he seen us?" she whispered, though there was no chance of them being heard.

"I don't—" Rand's response stuck in his throat as he recognized the lights on top of the SUV and the push bar on the front grille. "I think that's a deputy sheriff's vehicle."

"Really?"

When the SUV was a few hundred yards away, Rand was able to discern large orange lettering on the side.

"Does that say Sheriff?" He pointed.

"I...can't read it. The last letter looks to be an *F*."

"Like in sheriff," Rand said.

Kate promptly broke into a wide, glorious smile. "We're saved."

"Yeah." He smiled back at her. "We are."

"Girls! Eb!" Kate made a funnel of her hands and shouted. "Good news. A deputy sheriff is coming this way."

Hope gave her a fresh burst of energy. She forgot about her aching muscles and gnawing hunger.

"Brie, Brie," Serene shrieked. "We're saved."

Eb gave out a whoop.

"We're coming," Serene said.

"No, wait for me," she instructed. "I'll be right there." Eb would need help.

"You go," Rand pushed to his feet and then helped Kate. "I'll run and intercept the deputy before he gets away."

"Okay. Okay." She squeezed his hand.

His tender expression told her he understood. This would all be worth it when they got out of here.

As she eased her legs over the ravine's edge, she watched Rand striding forward at an awkward jog. *Please let him reach the SUV before it passes by.* Maybe Kate should have been the one to chase after the deputy.

Another thought occurred to her. The deputy could well be looking for them. Surely, someone had contacted the sheriff's department to report them missing. Murry and Scotty would have called the ranch once they reached a place where their phones had reception. Eb's employer might have reported him missing, too.

She'd assumed the rain had delayed any rescue efforts. Yet here was a deputy sheriff, come to their aid. How, she wondered, had he known to look for them in this remote spot? They were miles from the campsite.

Thank You, Lord, for this incredible blessing. We are so grateful.

"Kate," Serene hollered from the bottom of the ravine. "What's taking so long? This Eb dude's leg started bleeding again."

"Badly?"

"I don't know."

"I'm fine," Eb called. "Don't listen to her."

Serene did have a tendency to exaggerate, and Eb had said he was fine.

"I'll be right there. Rand's flagging down the deputy sheriff."

A glance his way confirmed he was making progress. The SUV appeared to have stopped. He must have seen Rand. Thank goodness.

She started to lower herself over the ravine's edge when a movement in the mountains to her left startled her. Unless she was seeing things, the woman hiker moved through the brush and cacti. Kate had to alert Rand. The woman also needed rescuing.

Except when she glanced back in Rand's direction, he was gone! The SUV remained where it was, crawling along the maintenance road. But there was no sign of Rand.

Where was he? Had he fallen? Was he hurt?

Fear crashed through her. "Rand. Rand!"

Suddenly, she saw him lying flat on the ground.

"What happened? Rand? Rand!"

He didn't answer. A second later, she saw why. From

out of nowhere, a lone ATV materialized from the opposite direction. It drove straight for the deputy sheriff's SUV.

One of the miners! She'd recognize the dark clothing and helmet anywhere.

This made no sense. Why would an illegal miner approach a deputy sheriff?

From where she clung to the edge of the ravine, Kate watched as the SUV rolled to a stop not a hundred feet away. The ATV pulled right up beside the SUV and parked. With the engine still running, the driver climbed off and approached the SUV. The driver's side door opened, and a uniformed man exited. The pair stood beside the hood and conversed, the miner gesturing and pointing. He made no effort to hide the rifle slung over his shoulder.

"What's taking so long?" Serene shouted from below. "Is the deputy coming for us?"

If Kate didn't answer, Serene would keep yelling. Praying no one heard her over idling engines, she called down. "Quiet, Serene. I'm not kidding."

"What—"

"Quiet."

Rand lifted his head slightly and fired a warning look back at Kate. She sent him an apologetic head shake.

The miner and the deputy sheriff talked for a good five minutes. During the entire time, Kate clutched the rocks she was holding with such force, her fingers cramped. Here they were, a short walk away from the man who killed the hiker and fired on Eb and the girls. If not him, then one of his equally dangerous cohorts.

Please, please, don't let them spot us.

Or the woman hiker. She was also innocent and had

suffered the loss of her companion. Kate harbored no doubts the miner would shoot any of them on sight.

The thought terrified her, and she began to tremble. Even more frightening was the prospect that the deputy was in cahoots with the miners. Someone who should be protecting them was a criminal.

Wait, no. Kate drew in a calming breath. She was getting carried away. The deputy sheriff probably had no idea the man was an illegal miner. He was likely giving him a warning about driving a motorized vehicle in the mountains.

Except the miner had driven straight toward the deputy sheriff and carried his rifle on full display.

Unease turned to dread. Something wasn't right here.

"Kate?" Serene's voice came softer now.

Before she could warn Serene to be quiet, the miner returned to his ATV. He and the deputy sheriff drove off in separate directions.

Thank You, Lord. Thank You, thank You.

They were alive. She watched the ATV disappear the way it had come—passing too close to Rand for comfort. He'd been smart to suggest they wear their bright yellow ponchos on the inside. His brown jacket blended with the ground and camouflaged him.

How soon until either the miner or the deputy sheriff returned? They needed to get out of here fast.

She waited, not daring to move. Rand would return when he was certain it was safe for him to do so.

Seconds ticked by. She considered going back to the girls and Eb but didn't want to leave Rand out there alone.

"Kate," Serene called in a scared voice. "The creek's getting really high."

Kate couldn't see it well through the trees, but she could hear the sound of rushing water, louder than before. "I'm waiting for Rand."

"What about the deputy?" Serene asked.

"He's gone."

"Is he sending back help?"

Kate didn't want to alarm the girls and Eb until she was with them and had a chance to explain. "Hang tight."

Rand struggled to his feet and jogged back toward her, crouching low. Rather than climb back down, Kate pulled herself up and out of the ravine. When he reached her, he dropped to his knees. Kate didn't hesitate and wrapped him in a fierce hug. They'd survived another terrifying encounter, and she needed his reassuring presence.

"You're all right." Her words came out in a rush.

He returned her hug, holding her close. Surely, he must hear her racing heart.

"Oh, Rand. I can't believe it. The miner almost saw us."

"But he didn't."

She released him then and examined the gash on his face. "Does that hurt?"

He wiped at the blood on his cheek with the back of his hand. "It's nothing."

Not nothing, but not life-threatening.

"The girls are scared," she said. "Eb's leg is bleeding again, and the water's rising."

"Kate." His intense gaze held hers. "I think the miners are in partnership with the deputy. They looked pretty chummy."

"I thought that, too."

"The meeting had to be arranged. What other reason would the deputy have to be out here in this storm?"

"He wasn't looking for us. Not to rescue us, anyway."

"No, he wasn't," Rand agreed. "And if you think about it, the miners need someone on the take in law enforcement. Thousands of people visit the Superstition Mountains every year. Not all of them to this area, but enough that carrying out an illegal mining operation is impossible unless you have help. Someone to cover for them and give them inside information and warn them of trouble."

"If that's true," Kate said, her mind jumping ahead, "then we're in even more danger than before."

Rand gripped her hand in his. "We need a new plan."

"I think I saw the woman hiker earlier."

"I saw her, too."

"Is she following us?"

"Following or watching us. Either one."

Kate peered down into the ravine and through the trees, searching for the girls and Eb. "We should hurry."

"You first. I'm right behind you."

She started down, scooting on her backside. Her jeans were soaked and filthy. It couldn't be avoided. The sound of rushing water when they entered the trees was deafening. The creek had risen another foot in the time she and Rand were gone and resembled a small river.

Serene burst through the trees. "Hurry. Eb needs help."

They found him and Brie at the water's edge. He sat with his back against a log. His legs were in the water well past his knees. Brie stood behind him, clinging to a branch.

"I didn't want to leave him," she said in a thin voice.

Rand got to Eb ahead of Kate. "Are you okay?"

"Been better. We were getting kind of worried." The older man indicated the creek and the swift current tugging at his legs. "Water's rising fast."

"We told you," Serene said defensively.

"You did." Kate silently berated herself. Why hadn't she hurried? Eb could have drowned. "How's your leg, Eb?"

"I've been applying pressure."

"We tried to carry him," Brie added. "He was too heavy."

"Going to have to go on that keto diet when I get home." His chuckle turned into a wheeze.

Rand bent and took hold of the older man's arm. Kate grabbed his other one. Together, they hauled Eb out of the water and to his feet.

Another thirty minutes, and the fast-moving current would have sucked him under. Nature could be as treacherous as it was beautiful. In less than a day, a trickle of water in the ravine bottom had morphed into a deadly danger.

"I'm sorry," Kate told Eb. "Really sorry. I had no idea."

"Don't go blaming yourself. Talking to the deputy sheriff was more important than babysitting me. Did he say how long until help arrives?"

"That's the thing." She hated having to tell them. "We never talked to him."

"You didn't? Why not?"

"One of the miners made a surprise appearance," Rand said.

He didn't go into details, and Kate didn't blame him. There'd be time for that later.

Eb hung his head, the light of hope in his eyes dimming.

"We're not going to be rescued?" Serene started to cry.

Brie was already in tears.

"Hey," Kate said. "Don't cry. Don't panic. Everything will be fine."

"We need to get out of here." Rand hitched his chin at the raging water.

"Right. Let me check Eb's bandage first."

Fortunately, the bleeding wasn't too bad. After re-tightening the tourniquet—all she could in their current circumstances—they began walking. To avoid the rising water, they had to walk closer to the ravine wall where the ground slanted at a sharp angle.

Eb leaned heavily against Rand. Kate suspected the older man's leg hurt more than he was letting on.

When they stopped to rest, Kate asked Rand, "What's the new plan?"

"We stay in the ravine. At least until dark. I get it won't be easy, but it's our only choice. We have to remain hidden, and the miners will avoid the water."

Serene suddenly shrieked. "Look!"

They turned to see a swell of water three feet high rolling down the length of the river like a miniature tsunami. The flash flood they'd worried about had arrived, and they needed to get out of the way now!

Chapter Eleven

"Is everyone okay?"

Rand leaned against the ravine wall, his chest heaving. He held on to Eb, who slumped over with his eyes closed.

"I'm getting a little tired of these close calls."

"Me, too, buddy." Rand looked past him to Kate. "How are you and the girls?"

She held them, one under each arm. She, too, was catching her breath. "All right. More shaken than anything else."

"How about we just wait here a minute?" Rand said. "Figure out what's next."

Where there had once been a creek, a full-fledged river raged. Its width had expanded to swallow brush and the lower half of the trees. A corridor of about five feet wide remained between the tree line and the ravine wall. The uneven ground slanted at a forty-five-degree angle. The going would be demanding for physically fit individuals. For them, it would be a challenge like none other they'd previously faced.

They were spent, scared and shaking. They were also

alive. Had Rand and Kate waited any longer before re-joining Eb and the girls, their dead bodies might now be floating down the river.

"I'm hungry," Serene said.

Who could think of food right now? A twelve-year-old girl, apparently.

"We all are," Rand said, though, in truth, his stomach had twisted into a tight knot, squashing any sensation of hunger. For the moment. He'd feel different when they were out of danger.

Bracing a hand on the boulder beside him, he pushed off. The effort cost him most of the strength he had left. "I got a good look around earlier. There's only about ten or twelve more miles to the trailhead."

"That's a lot," Brie said softly.

"It is. If we walk at night, alongside the ravine rather than in it, we'll make better time. I still think the miners are less likely to come looking for us in the dark."

"Less likely," Serene grumbled, "not unlikely."

"We can't stay here."

"That's not what you said a few minutes ago."

"All right, Serene," Kate chided her. "Enough's enough. I get it. You're scared and hungry and tired. We all are. Snapping at Rand won't improve our situation."

"Sorry."

Rand gave her a nod. "Don't worry about it." He had bigger problems to deal with than a grumpy kid.

"We can't lose hope," Kate said. "Ten or twelve miles seems like a lot. But we could be home by tomorrow if we keep moving."

"Can't we find a cave like before and wait there until someone finds us?" Brie asked. "I'm really tired."

Rand could relate. Between the storm and the gunshot and guard duty, none of them had slept well that first night at camp. They'd barely slept a wink last night.

"We'll take frequent breaks," he said. "I promise." He glanced at the sky. "Hard as it is, we're better off traveling at night to evade the miners."

Hearing a loud crack, they turned to see the rushing water snatch a branch clean off a tree and carry it away.

"Oh, wow," Kate said.

Rand helped Eb to stand straight. "That's our cue to leave."

Poor Eb wobbled more than the last time and nearly pitched forward. Rand wondered how much more he had in him. Those ten or twelve miles might as well be a hundred if Eb wasn't able to continue. Then what? They couldn't abandon him, which meant someone had to stay behind with him.

"Can you make it, pal?" Rand asked.

"Wouldn't mind a little help from above right about now." He offered a wan smile.

"We can always ask." Rand didn't hesitate and began to pray aloud. Not caring about the rain and their discomfort, he let the words come from his heart. "Dear Lord. For whatever reason, we are on this difficult path. Even with all the trials we've faced and will continue to face, we feel Your presence with us. We ask that You continue to protect us from the miners as You have so far and give us the strength we need to carry on. We implore You to send the miners away. Let them believe we are no longer a threat to them. Keep us shielded from their view so that we remain safe and can return home to our loved ones. Guide us in the right direction and give us the wisdom to choose wisely. A break in the weather would be nice, too, if You can manage that," he added on a lighter note. "We are Your humble servants, Lord, this day and always. Amen."

A chorus of amens echoed his, some soft, some clear.

Rand raised his head to find four anxious faces staring at him. They were counting on him and his expertise to lead them out of the mountains. And he would give everything he had to ensure that happened. God was also counting on Rand to do His work, as He should. Rand was familiar with the mountains. He knew the way to the trailhead. He was determined and filled with purpose, if weak of body.

Ten years ago, when the doctors had informed Rand he would never walk again, he had refused to believe them. He'd persevered and proved the doctors wrong. He'd persevere now, too.

As would Kate. She'd survived difficult circumstances. They were alike in that way. In other ways, too, Rand was beginning to realize.

"Okay, here's the plan. It won't be dark for another hour. Until then, we keep to this narrow corridor. It won't be easy, but we can do it. Then, as soon as it's dark, we climb out of the ravine and continue alongside it. Depending on how far we get, and if we find a decent shelter, we can stop and rest for a few hours."

Kate looked unconvinced. "I'm worried about Eb. I'm not sure he can—"

"I'll be fine," he said, cutting her off. "You worry about the girls."

"What if we don't reach the trailhead by morning? If we're not rescued soon, we're going to be in serious trouble."

She wasn't wrong. Lack of food was having an effect on them. Intense physical exertion, combined with their bodies' efforts to keep warm, was burning valuable calories at an alarming rate. Without replenishing those calories, they wouldn't last long. And Eb was in the worst shape of all of them. Age, pain and loss of blood were draining him.

He attempted a chuckle. "A little divine intervention would be nice."

"Yes it would," Rand concurred. "For now, we walk. As long as we're making progress, we have a chance. Staying here, giving up, is a death sentence."

His blunt words had the desired effect. Everyone mustered their courage and fortitude and set out. God must have listened to their prayers, for they heard no more engines. And while the water continued to rise, there wasn't another surge.

Rand didn't allow himself to become overconfident, however. They had a long trek ahead of them.

They stopped to rest every twenty minutes. Rand doubted they'd covered more than a mile in the last hour. Eb slowed them down considerably. He knew it, too.

"This is a pretty nice boulder," he said when they reached a particularly treacherous curve. "How about I rest my weary bones, and you all continue without me? I'll be waiting right here when that help of yours finally arrives."

"We're not leaving you," Kate insisted.

He conceded. But during the next rest break, they had an almost identical conversation. Eb was losing the will to continue. The girls, too. Evening fell all around them, adding to their discouragement.

Gray, gloomy shadows darkened to black. Time slowed. Steps became a laser-focused series of one foot in front of the other. Rand resumed the lead, half carrying Eb. The girls and Kate lagged behind. *Don't fall*, he told himself. *Don't slip. Don't let them down.*

As he trudged along, his thoughts bounced from one random memory to another. His first rodeo. A childhood birthday party. Ansel praying with him in the hospital. Was it yesterday or the day before when he and Kate had sat together in the cave and talked about starting fresh?

"What was that?" Kate asked.

Rand stopped short and almost lost his balance. At the jarring motion, Eb's head snapped up. It had been lolling since the last rest break.

"What was what?" Rand asked. He hadn't heard anything. Then again, he'd been on automatic pilot and not paying attention.

"I swear I heard a horse whinny." Kate tilted her head as if to hear better.

"You sure?" He thought she was imagining. Or maybe hallucinating. They could be that far gone.

"Listen."

He did, expecting nothing. But then he heard it, too. Not a whinny, but rather the steady clip-clop of hooves on loose, wet ground. Multiple horses. Very close by. Right above their heads. He became instantly alert.

"Stay here while I check it out."

"I'll go with you."

Rand shook his head before she could plead her case. "Not this time, Kate. And I mean it. You need to take care of the girls and Eb."

"All right."

Climbing out of the ravine required considerable effort. Rand's legs no longer hurt. They were numb. He wasn't sure that was a good or bad thing. Dragging himself over the edge on his belly, he fell facefirst into the dirt. After a moment, he lifted his head. Tiny slivers of moonlight penetrated the cloud cover, allowing him to make out shapes. He looked left. Nothing in that direction resembling a miner.

Hearing a nicker, he turned right. Large, dim forms materialized not twenty feet from him. The herd of wild horses! Impossible but true. They stood in a tight cluster. The one in front, lighter colored than the rest, stared almost as if it had been expecting him. Peeking out from behind it was a colt, four or five months old at most.

What were they doing here? Following Rand and the others? He wanted to say that made no sense. Except incredible things happened every day. Hadn't he walked again when the doctors predicted he'd spend the rest of his life in a wheelchair?

"Tell me," he said to the lead horse, "are you tame?"

It continued to stare at him, tail swishing.

He stared back. The idea of capturing one of them was insane. Except, there they stood. Unmoving.

"Rand?" Kate called. "What do you see?"

"The wild horses. They're here."

He expected the herd to bolt at the sound of human voices. They didn't. The lead horse shook its head, ruffling its shaggy mane.

Could he catch this horse? If he was going to try, now was the time. Eb could ride the horse while the rest of them walked alongside. They'd cover a lot more miles in less time.

Six horses. Twenty feet away. Rand had to decide and fast.

God, please let at least one of them be tame.

The lead horse cranked its big head around and

looked back at the remaining herd. Rand saw it then in the pale, pale light. A white freeze brand on the horse's left shoulder. He was sure of it. This horse had once belonged to someone. And it wasn't afraid of them.

"Kate," Rand called, feeling his excitement escalate. "Get up here."

"What about Eb and the girls?"

"Put Serene in charge. This is important. And hurry. We're only going to have one shot at this, and we need to make it count."

Kate stood beside Rand, utterly captivated and afraid if she so much as blinked, the small herd would scatter.

Six horses faced them, ears pricked forward, tails swishing from side to side. She still didn't believe it.

"They aren't running away," she whispered.

"No."

"Why is that?"

"I have no idea." Rand shook his head.

"What should we do? Just walk over to them?"

"Wish I had a carrot or a bucket of grain."

"You first," Kate said. "If both of us go, they'll spook."

"No. You first. You're smaller than me. Less threatening."

"Right." Her legs shook with excitement and apprehension. She must not, *could* not, blow this.

"Easy, Kate. Take your time. We've got all night."

His soothing voice eased her nervousness. The horses', too. She locked gazes with the lead one. There had to be a reason why the herd had been following them all day. Something greater than mere coincidence.

Kate believed in free will. She also believed God

placed opportunities in front of people and gave them the choice to act or do nothing. Embrace or ignore.

She would embrace.

"Hey, you," she said softly. "What's your name?"

The lead horse bobbed its head and snorted. The young colt pressed against its side, seeking reassurance.

"Are you a mom? Is that your baby?"

The horse bent its head and nuzzled the colt.

"I'd say yes. Well, you don't have to worry. We won't hurt him. Or any of you."

Kate inched closer.

"I'm going to call you Sugar because you're so sweet. You like that?"

Feeling braver and calmer, she took two more steps. Sugar just kept staring at her, her hide twitching. She seemed more curious than wary. Behind her, the other horses shifted anxiously. All at once, the colt squealed and broke away. He circled the herd before returning to the mare's side, his feet dancing in place.

"You have a lot of energy, baby. Haven't seen people up close before, have you? Don't you worry. I'm nice."

By now, only six feet separated Kate from the horses. Her legs continued to shake despite her efforts to relax. Taking a chance, she reached out a hand to Sugar, palm exposed and nonthreateningly.

The mare stretched her head out and sniffed.

"That's a good girl."

Sugar's nostrils quivered as if she was testing Kate's scent.

"We need your help. You remember what it was like to be ridden, don't you?"

The mare pawed the ground.

Kate advanced another two steps. Was she taking too long or going too fast? Would Sugar bolt?

"Don't rush her," Rand said. He hadn't moved.

"I won't." Kate slowed her breathing and concentrated on her outstretched hand. "We have two girls with us. They're twelve and can be a real pain in the neck sometimes. You get it. You're a mom and know how kids are. Eb is our friend. He tried to help us and now he's hurt. Walking's really hard for him. It would be nice if he could ride for a while. Just as far as the trailhead."

Sugar nickered and bobbed her rangy head.

Two more steps, and only inches separated Kate and Sugar. The other horses backed up. The paint pinned its ears back and bared its teeth. The colt spun and presented his hind end, his back feet striking out in little kicks. But the horses didn't run away. They wouldn't without their leader, Sugar. Their herding instincts were too strong. If Kate could somehow lead Sugar to the ravine, the remaining horses would follow.

And if she could ride Sugar…

Curiosity must have won out, for the mare lifted a hoof and planted it on the ground in front of her, bringing herself a few inches closer to Kate.

"Yes! Keep coming."

Sugar advanced another step.

"Aren't you a good girl," Kate singsonged and then swallowed a gasp when Sugar's velvety nose brushed her palm.

Don't move. Don't breathe. Don't scare her.

She waited to see what Sugar would do next. To her astonishment, the mare walked forward and into Kate's open arms.

She broke into sobs and stroked the horse's neck. "You sweet, sweet girl. You are special. A lifesaver. You know that?"

"Well done, Kate," Rand said. "You think you can lead her over here?"

"I can do better than that." Kate couldn't explain it; she just knew that Sugar would be okay with what she planned next.

Carefully, she lowered one hand to the fanny pack at her waist and removed it. That accomplished, she gently looped the straps around Sugar's neck and fastened the buckle. The result was a rudimentary reining device.

"See." She scratched Sugar between the ears. "That wasn't so bad."

The colt had a different opinion and pranced in place.

Gathering her courage, Kate grabbed a thick hank of mane in her left hand, and, in a single swift move learned from her junior rodeo days, swung herself up and onto Sugar's back. The mare briefly jerked in surprise but quickly settled. Clutching the fanny pack strap, Kate used her legs to urge Sugar into a walk.

Rand beamed at her. "You are incredible, Kate Spencer."

"Sugar deserves all the credit."

"Not all of it."

Kate basked in his praise. Using her legs and the strap, she guided Sugar in a figure-eight pattern. The mare responded as if she'd never left the ranch where she must have once lived. She plodded along slowly, displaying a docile temperament and willingness to please.

Thank You, Lord, for this marvelous gift.

The other horses followed parallel to Sugar, not too

close, not too far. Her colt trotted along beside her. He wasn't sure about Kate, but he wasn't leaving his mama.

When Kate brought the mare to a standstill in front of Rand, he held out his hand like Kate had done to let Sugar smell him. She did and made no objection when he traced the outline of her freeze brand with his fingers.

"I named her Sugar," Kate announced.

"It fits."

"You think one of the other horses might also be tame enough to ride?"

"We can always find out."

"Or we quit while we're ahead. Eb can ride Sugar. That alone will make a big difference."

Rand considered the rest of the herd. "That old swayback over there has some potential."

"Are you nuts? He looks ready to stomp you into the dirt."

"We'll see."

Rand proved his skill with handling horses. Ten minutes later, he was running his hand along the swayback's withers.

"If he hasn't been ridden before, he's just got his first lesson."

"You're just showing off," Kate teased.

"I can't be outdone by a girl."

"Is your ego that fragile?"

"Watch and learn."

"Rand, you can't just break a horse like that."

"This guy is old as the hills and lame. He won't put up a fight."

Rand undid his belt and, similar to what Kate had done with her fanny pack, looped it around the swayback's neck. The swayback snorted angrily and attempted to retreat, tripping over his enormous feet.

"Whoa. Easy, boy. That's right."

Kate walked Sugar to stand near the swayback in hopes the mare's proximity would help settle him. It did.

"You're a fine old fellow." Rand stroked the horse's head. "We're going to be friends, you and I."

Before the horse had a chance to realize what was happening, Rand was sitting on his back. Startled, the swayback shuffled his feet and then gave a token buck. Rand let him huff and puff for a minute, then cued the swayback to walk.

"That's right, partner. Good job."

He brought the horse to a stop across from Kate and Sugar. The remaining four horses watched with visible agitation. They'd never seen anything like this and expressed their dislike by darting off, only to return and paw the ground. The colt reared on his hind legs, mimicking the dominance he'd one day show as a stallion defending his herd. Through it all, Sugar and the swayback remained blessedly calm.

"What now?" Kate asked Rand.

"We ride out with these two. The rest are too wild."

"Should we continue following the ravine?"

Rand nodded. "We could too easily lose our way in the dark."

"One thing in our favor," Kate added. "The miners won't be looking for us on horseback."

"True." Rand turned the swayback around. "Now for the hard part. Let's get Eb and the girls."

Serene was already climbing out of the ravine when they neared. Kate suspected she'd been watching them the whole time.

"You have the horses!"

"No running," Rand warned.

"Can I ride, too?"

"Not yet."

He dismounted and adjusted the belt to a better position. The swayback responded well, already accepting his new role of trail horse. Rand motioned to Serene.

"Come here. Very slowly."

She did as instructed, and Rand made the introductions. Serene was more delighted with the swayback than he was with her. When the horse seemed ready, he had Serene take hold of the belt.

"You wait here with him and Kate. I'm going down for Brie and Eb."

"Okay." Serene nodded vigorously and stared at her hand holding on to the belt with wonderment.

"I'm counting on you," Rand said. "We all are."

Kate thought the girl's spine might have straightened a little with determination and pride.

He then gestured to Kate. "Bring Sugar over so this old guy feels more secure."

Sugar was pleased to oblige. She and the colt were both happier standing next to their herd mate. Rand gave them a final inspection before returning to the ravine.

After what felt like an hour, but was probably more like fifteen minutes, Brie crawled out. She walked slowly toward them. Rand must have warned her.

She stopped fifteen feet away, her expression alight. "That is so cool."

Kate had to smile. She patted Sugar's neck. "It is."

Soon after that, Rand and Eb made their way out of the ravine. Both men limped; Eb clearly was worse for the wear.

"How you doing, Eb?" Kate asked.

"Fully recharged and ready to go." The strain on his face belied his jovial tone.

He wasn't the only one in rough shape, thought Kate. They were a pitiful lot, all of them sporting injuries, from cuts and scrapes to sprains and bruises. They were fortunate no one had fallen and broken a bone like Cayden back at camp.

Rand's gaze met Kate's, and his expression softened. The connection she'd previously felt passed between them again. She knew without a doubt their growing fondness for each other wasn't temporary, the result of being in danger. It was real and would continue.

Kate's spirits rocketed. They had overcome every obstacle. Kept going when others would have given up. Come tomorrow, they would ride out of these mountains on the beautiful, wonderful horses God had sent to them.

At last, the worst was over.

Chapter Twelve

"We'll ride double," Rand said. "Kate, you and Brie take the swayback. Serene and Eb, you two are on Sugar." He turned to face Serene. "Can you handle the horse with Eb riding behind you?"

Though Kate had bonded with the mare, she was the most experienced rider next to Rand. Serene, despite her feisty attitude, was no match for a green broke horse. Even a very old one with knobby arthritic knees. The swayback required someone of Kate's abilities.

"Absolutely." The girl straightened her spine.

She had confidence; Rand would give her that.

"Good, because I'm counting on you."

"What about you?" Kate asked from atop Sugar.

"I'll stay here. Wait for you to send help."

"No!"

"The trailhead isn't far. You won't be long."

"I don't know the way," she protested.

"Eb does."

The older man gave a mild shrug.

"Those horses are wild." Kate's voice rose. "We need

you, Rand. What if one of us gets bucked off? We have no saddles or bridles."

Rand rubbed his forehead. He had never met a more obstinate woman.

"Stop arguing with me, Kate, and think about it. Nothing else makes sense. The horses can't carry more than two adults. Not for long and not through this terrain. You said yourself, they're wild."

"I'll stay behind," Eb said. "I'm mostly useless anyway."

Kate groaned. "What is wrong with you guys? We already agreed, we stay together. No one being left behind."

Rand tried another approach. "My legs hurt. I need the rest."

"Then I'll stay, and you go."

Okay, that backfired. Rand tried again.

"I'm the best choice. I know the area and can find a place to hide where the miners won't look for me. I have the endurance to last until help arrives. Which will be tomorrow."

"You'd leave us to fend for ourselves?"

"I'm improving your chances of making it out of here by not holding you back."

"You and Eb. You're a pair." Kate slid off the mare without letting go of the fanny pack strap. She faced Rand. "We're all leaving. I repeat, none of us is staying behind. You ride the swayback with Brie. I'll walk."

"I'll walk," Rand said.

"This isn't a contest. You said yourself, your legs hurt. Mine don't."

His temper got the best of him. "I'm not letting you—"

"I've had my fill of your giant ego. And if you keep

letting it get in the way, we'll never get out of here. All our efforts to capture the horses will be for nothing."

"No way you can keep up with the horses on foot." Rand was committed to winning this power struggle.

"I can. Better than you."

"You're being stubborn."

"I'm being sensible. Trust me. I'm not a martyr. Save the others." She gestured melodramatically. "Leave me behind. I'm expendable. I've been a bad person and deserve this." She dropped her arms. "The fact is I'm the best candidate. I can walk farther than you."

"You won't last a mile."

"After everything we've been through the last two days, I can't believe you said that. I'm a warrior."

Serene pumped the air with her fist. "You go, Miss Kate."

Rand wasn't ready to give up. "You'll stumble and fall."

"I'll hold on to Sugar's tail, and she can pull me along. You just need to go slow. If I get tired, one of the girls can relieve me for a short while."

He hated with every fiber of his being that what she said made sense. He also hated that she was right about his pride getting in the way. The sad truth was, Rand couldn't keep up. Jagged slivers of pain shot up and down his legs with each step he took. Unless he rested for the night, he'd be the one not lasting a mile. Maybe less.

As if reading his mind, Kate said, "I'd say let's spend the night in a shelter, but there's no way these horses will stick around. I don't care that they've been following us for a day. Not happening."

More logic. She was good at it.

"Promise me you'll say something if you're too tired to continue."

She nodded. "I will."

Reluctantly, he took hold of Eb's arm. "Ready? I'll give you a boost. Brie, I need you to hold on to the horse."

"Me?" she squeaked.

"You can do it."

Brie wrapped her fingers around the belt and giggled when the swayback sniffed her hair.

Above them, small slits appeared in the cloud covering, allowing pale moonlight to filter through. If not over, the storm was taking a break. In the darkness, the surrounding mountains reminded Rand of giant creatures from a scary childhood fable.

Nearby, the remaining four horses tossed their heads and whinnied their objections to what these humans were planning with their brethren. Coyotes yipped in the far distance. An owl hooted, warning intruders to stay away from his territory.

These weren't the only nocturnal creatures venturing out of hiding now that the rain had ceased. Rand remembered the mountain lion that had been seen near Still Water Ranch the other day. They were likely safe from him, their group too loud and noisy and intimidating.

Rand helped Eb onto Sugar. The older man grunted in pain as he grabbed hold of a clump of mane for leverage and swung his uninjured leg over the mare's back. Sitting up, he closed his eyes and breathed heavily.

"Give me a minute, okay?"

"Take your time, pal."

"How's his bandage?" Kate asked.

Rand checked. "It'll do until we reach home."

"Your turn, Serene." He gave the girl a leg up, sitting her in front of Eb. "Hold the fanny pack strap and grip with your knees. If you need to turn her right or left, move the strap like this." He demonstrated. "Give her a nudge with your heels if she's reluctant."

Sugar shifted and snorted, unsure about this new arrangement. Beside her, the colt danced nervously as if electricity ran through its slender legs.

"Easy does it, girl," Rand soothed and patted the mare's neck. After a moment, she calmed. "You okay, Serene?"

"Uh-huh."

"Yeah?"

She nodded.

Rand motioned. "All right, Brie. It's our turn."

Kate and the girl traded places, with Kate taking over the job of holding on to the swayback.

Rand still thought he should remain behind, but he was afraid—no, certain—Kate would refuse to go without him. And he doubted Eb and the girls could make it out on their own despite Eb knowing the way. Besides, the older man was in no shape to lead the expedition.

"Me first," he told Brie.

The old horse stood like a champ, easing Rand's worries. Once he sat comfortably astride, he extended his hand to Brie.

"Your turn."

With the four of them on horseback, and Kate on foot, they were ready.

"Where do we cross the wash?" Kate asked.

Rand looked around, trying to visualize the way to the trailhead. "The ravine splits into a Y about a half mile east of here. I think the water will be shallower there."

"And if it's not?"

"It will be. Plus, we have the horses. They're a lot stronger than we are."

"True." After a moment, she flashed a brave smile he suspected was for herself as much as the benefit of the others.

He understood her doubts. But what other choice did they have than to cross? Spending another night in the mountains wasn't an option. They'd barely eaten in days, and the miners were out there somewhere.

Lord, we are almost home. Walk with us during the rest of this difficult journey. Guide us. Bolster us. Protect us.

"We should get started," he said.

Kate stood behind Sugar. She gently patted the mare's hind end and cooed in a soft voice. When Sugar remained calm, Kate took hold of her long tail and combed her fingers through the thick stands of hair.

She nodded, swallowed and squared her shoulders. "Ready."

"Go on, Serene," Rand said.

The girl clucked and cued the mare to walk. Her colt trotted along beside her, intent on avoiding this strange being hanging on to his mama. Rand followed on the swayback. He kept his eyes focused on Kate, watching her every step. At the first sign of trouble, he'd bail off the swayback and rush to her.

They progressed slowly. The other horses ambled along, not too close, not too far away. They would not abandon their leader.

"How you doing, Serene?" Rand asked after a few minutes.

"Okay." Her answer sounded weak.

"You're amazing, kiddo. I'm proud of you."

They walked parallel to the ravine, tripling their previous rate of progress. Below them, the sound of raging water reminded them of the perilous crossing that lay ahead.

Time passed. No one talked. They were too busy concentrating on riding. To everyone's relief, there was no sign of the miners. Perhaps the deputy had warned them to leave the area.

The horses did well and responded to direction. Rand had been wrong about the distance. They'd traveled nearly two miles, and the ravine had yet to split in two.

"Kate, why don't we trade places?"

"I'm all right."

She wasn't. She'd stumbled several times now.

"After we cross," he said.

"We'll see."

He hated his disability. Yes, he was grateful for the mobility he had. But there were days when he'd give anything to have full use of his legs.

There but for the grace of God go I. Not a day went by Rand didn't tell himself that.

"Eb, what about you?" he asked.

"I'm managing."

"I recognize this peak. The ravine splits just ahead."

No one responded. He'd been wrong once already about the distance. He could be wrong again.

"It won't be far to the trailhead once we cross the wash," he said, attempting to raise everyone's spirits. "A few hours at most."

"Assuming these ponies will actually cross the wash," Eb said.

Eb wasn't joking, and nobody laughed. If the horses did refuse, which was a real possibility, they'd have to cross on their own.

At the place where the ravine diverged, Rand insisted on getting off the swayback and climbing down the ravine to locate a shallow crossing place. Though Kate wanted to go with him, she waited at the top with Eb and the girls, holding on to the swayback. Fortunately, the horses were content to stand quietly, having become somewhat used to humans.

She worried about Rand, if the climb was too much for him in his current depleted condition. But he wouldn't have it any other way.

His head appeared twenty minutes later, followed by the rest of him.

"Good news?" Kate asked.

He stood with visible difficulty and brushed away clumps of dirt clinging to his pant legs. "The water is five or six feet deep here. I think we'll find a shallower place a little farther along."

"You think?"

"I do."

"But you aren't sure?"

"You have a better plan?"

She didn't. And, like that, the decision was made.

Rand hesitated before mounting the swayback.

"Is there a problem?" Kate asked.

"Maybe it would be better if I lead him across."

This, thought Kate, wasn't the time for her to be delicate with her words. "Your legs aren't strong enough to battle the current. If the horse balks, Brie won't be able to control him. But you can."

Rand's response was to walk the swayback to a boulder, which he used as a mounting block. Much easier than pulling himself up onto the horse's back.

They traveled a short distance to a less steep incline that would be easier on the horses and less intimidating.

"I'll go first," Kate said. "Sugar will follow me."

She stood at the edge of the ravine, staring down at the racing water. The trees were thinner here, affording her a clear view. How could Rand be so sure of the water's depth? It could be four feet. Or six. Or eight. They might drown.

Rand and Serene also brought their horses to the edge. The remaining horses kept their distance. They didn't like the sound of rushing water and sensed danger. The swayback huffed and puffed. Only Rand's excellent horsemanship kept the swayback under control. Thank goodness. If he bolted, the others would, too.

"Be careful," Rand said after a moment. "If the mare gets going too fast, Serene won't be able to restrain her. Dive out of the way before she hurts you."

"I will."

"I want to walk down," Brie said in a small voice.

"Oh, honey," Kate said. "I know it's scary, thinking about riding down the incline. But once we're at the bottom, you may not be able to get back on. And you can't cross that river on your own."

Brie sniffed.

"Hold on to me and find your balance," Rand said. "Just like I taught you during riding lessons."

"We got this." Serene gave her foster sister a thumbs-up. "Aiesha is going to be so jealous when she hears."

Leave it to Serene to find the bright side.

Exhaling a long breath, Kate started down the ravine,

feeling for each step with her feet. Unlike before, she didn't need to slide on her hind end. The angle really was much less steep. Maybe the water was shallower.

"Careful, Serene," she cautioned when Sugar got too close and bumped Kate with her nose.

That wasn't Kate's only problem. The colt slipped, slid and scrambled, crashing into her and nearly sending her flying.

"I'm trying," Serene complained. "Rand's right behind me and upsetting Sugar."

And behind him were the other three horses. Gravity was their enemy, compelling the horses to pick up speed. Added to that, myriad hooves rained a mini avalanche of rocks and debris down on Kate. If she stepped out of the way, however, the horses would likely come to a stop. She had no choice but to continue.

Finally, thankfully, she reached the ravine bottom and jumped out of the way. Just in the nick of time. Six anxious horses charged ahead, glad to be on level ground. There, the rushing river brought them to an abrupt stop as if it were liquid fire rather than water.

"Everyone all right?" Rand asked.

Eb chuckled. "That was exciting."

Kate was thinking of a different word.

"We made it," Serene crowed triumphantly. She had a lot to be proud of, having done an incredible job.

Sugar's sides heaved, and she bobbed her head. Her colt whinnied, lost his footing and kicked out at another horse as he righted himself. The herd was eager to leave—the area as well as the humans.

"So, where's this shallower place you have in mind?" Kate asked Rand.

"About a hundred yards ahead. We'll walk along the

bank. That'll give the horses a chance to get used to the water."

His reasoning made sense.

This time, Kate went last. The terrain in this part of the ravine was indeed different, and there wasn't much room to maneuver. She had no desire to be trampled.

It didn't take long to reach the place Rand had picked out for them. The horses obliged by walking in a mostly calm line, except for the colt. It really was amazing how quickly they'd grown accustomed to people. And their herding instincts were a big help.

When Kate saw how much wider the ravine was, she felt better about Rand's prediction. That was until she approached the water's edge.

"This looks deep."

"It's because the water's moving fast," he said.

She studied Sugar's side. Rand had estimated four feet. That would bring the water to past the mare's shoulder. Horses waded or even swam through deep water all the time. But that was usually a pond or lazily flowing river. Not this natural disaster waiting to happen.

"Are you sure about this?" She met Rand's gaze from where he sat atop the swayback. In the dark, his eyes were the color of ink. "People die in flash floods. It happens all the time."

"No," he admitted with brutal honesty. "I'm not sure. The last two days aren't anything I've ever experienced before. But I believe this is our best chance."

"We could still walk out. Civilization isn't that far."

"You're right. If we can last that long and aren't shot at by the miners."

Kate wavered.

"Your call," he said, his tone kind and exerting no pressure. "If you don't want to cross, we won't."

"Give me a moment."

Lord, I need Your guidance now more than ever. Five lives are at stake. Which is the best course to take? Cross the wash or continue walking?

She waited for a sense of rightness telling her what to do. She remembered something Rosario had told her during a prison worship service about having to make choices. She'd said, "Leave the emotion out of it and trust in the Lord."

At the moment, Kate was feeling fear. If she removed that emotion and acted solely on logic, what would her choice be? She knew the answer. She'd cross the wash. Horses were large and strong and able to swim. The wash was only twelve feet across at its widest. They could make it.

She opened her eyes and met each person's anxious gaze. "What about the rest of you?"

"We cross," Serene said, sounding suddenly older.

Brie nodded, though Kate suspected she was just going along with Serene.

"I could have waded across and back by now," Eb joked.

Kate walked over to Rand, relieved when the swayback paid her no heed. She reached up, and he took her outstretched hand in his.

"Is this a yes?" he asked.

"Yes." She squeezed his fingers. "We cross." When she went to withdraw her hand, he refused to let go.

"I think you should ride Sugar with Serene and Eb."

"That's too much weight. The horse'll be pulled under."

He didn't answer. He didn't like that Kate was right.

What happened next was unexpected and achingly sweet. Rand leaned down, brought Kate's hand to his lips and placed a tender kiss on her palm.

"You're amazing," he said. "I should have returned your phone calls years ago."

"You weren't ready. And maybe I wasn't, either."

"I'm really glad you came to Still Water Ranch."

"Me, too."

"Good grief, you guys." Serene harrumphed. "Pu-leeze."

Kate grinned and made her way back to Sugar. "Keep your eyes straight ahead," she told the girl. "Focus on the opposite bank. Don't worry about anybody or anything else. Both you girls hold on tight no matter what happens. You hear me?"

"Got it."

She rested a hand on Sugar's muscular hind end and collected the mare's long tail in both her hands. This feat would require every ounce of her strength.

"Ready," she said and murmured another prayer.

Inch by inch, they headed into the river. Sugar refused at first. She lowered her head and pawed the water. Serene clucked and kicked the mare's sides, to no avail. Kate turned sideways, leaned her shoulder into Sugar's hind end and pushed, hoping she wouldn't get kicked. After a moment, Sugar advanced. The water instantly rose to meet them. Her startled and confused colt leaped in after his mother, his front legs instinctively churning.

Kate shivered when the cold water reached her boots and then soaked the bottom half of her pants. She concentrated on the back of Serene's head and the girl's long hair. Then, just like that, they were approaching the mid-point.

Rand spoke to all the horses, a point of calm in the chaos surrounding them. "Easy does it. That's right."

The fierce current sucked Kate down and shoved her hard to the right. Her feet skimmed over the slippery rocks, only to become trapped between two boulders. As she wrenched herself free, pain exploded in her right ankle, the one she'd twisted earlier. Her breath came in rapid bursts. Her fingers ached from the strain, yet she refused to let go of Sugar's tail.

Before Kate could regain her balance, she abruptly went down, sinking past her chest. She screamed as she instinctively kicked out with her legs. Where was the ravine bottom? Flailing, she sucked in water and began to cough.

Stand up, her mind shouted.

"Kate!" Rand hollered and tried to turn the sway-back. The horse was having none of it and fought hard to stay on course. "Kate. Answer me!"

The herd acted as one. They were a force to be reckoned with and refused to stop. Once in the water, they were determined to get across.

Kate fought and, amazingly, regained her footing. The vicious current could have toppled a concrete pillar. That she'd bested it was unbelievable.

"I'm okay."

She had no time to rest. Sugar plowed ahead. Serene's attempts to slow the mare were useless. Neither was Rand in control of the swayback. All around Kate, the other horses drove their large bodies through the water in a frenzied panic.

The colt struggled to stay with Sugar. Lighter than

the other horses, it drifted several feet away. Sugar became crazed and veered in an attempt to go after her baby, her legs chopping through the water like pistons. Frustrated, she started to buck.

Serene yelped, and Eb reached around her to grab the fanny pack straps. His legs might be useless but not his arms.

The paint horse reached the opposite bank first. This incensed the rest, and they were suddenly in a race to join him.

Brie screamed. "Help."

Kate could hardly see. Water splashed her in the face. Her hair, or Sugar's tail, fell in her eyes. "Don't stop," she yelled. Their only chance, *her* only chance, was to reach the other side.

Her fingers slipped, and she lost her grip on Sugar's tail. The mare charged ahead. Kate panicked.

"Rand!"

He appeared beside her on the swayback. She reached for him and missed. And missed again.

"I got her," Brie called.

Kate felt herself being hauled up by her jacket collar. It was enough. She was able to regain her footing.

"Don't let go of her," Rand shouted.

The swayback moved too fast, and Kate went momentarily under. She dog-paddled and was able to surface. But not for long. The current's grasp on her was too fierce.

Brie started to slide off the horse. She shrieked and flailed. As the girl's instinct to survive kicked in, she let go of Kate and reached for Rand, attempting to right herself. If she didn't, all three would be in the water and the swayback long gone.

Kate had to do something. Now!

Adrenaline pumping through her veins, she fought her way back to the swayback's side. There, she grabbed Brie by the seat of her pants and boosted the girl back up onto the horse. Her arm bones threatened to shatter, but she didn't quit. She kept shoving and shoving until the swayback barreled ahead and beyond Kate's reach.

She saw Brie center herself just as the horse made it to the opposite bank with the rest of the herd. She and Rand were safe on solid ground. Serene and Eb, too. Kate alone stood in the water, up to her thighs. Though the current remained strong, the water was shallower. She could walk out.

Rand hopped off the swayback. "Kate! Hurry."

He started for her, his boots hitting the water's edge.

She took a step—right into a hole. She stumbled and sank up to her neck. Before she knew what was happening, the current swept her away like a dry stick. She thrashed, trying to swim. The water carried her toward a branch hanging over the water. She tried to grab it. Her fingers met only thin air. A hard whack to the back of her head had her seeing stars.

The last thing she heard was the girls screaming and Rand shouting her name. After that, the water claimed her, and the world went black.

Chapter Thirteen

"Kate! Kate!" Rand jumped into the water, heedless of the danger. Hands seized his arms and held him in place before he could wade farther in. "Where are you?" He called her name over and over until his throat felt raw. *"No!"*

This couldn't be happening. He had to go after her. Save her. She was weak from exhaustion and hunger and no match for the racing current.

Someone, and then another someone, hauled him to the bank. Rand resisted and almost got away. His boot heel caught on a rock, and his legs went out from under him. He landed like a heavy sack of grain. Serene and Brie fell on top of him.

Pressure built inside his chest, stopping his heart from beating.

Kate. Kate. Kate. He'd lost her. The wash had carried her away.

"What are you thinking?" Serene rolled off him and clutched at his jacket sleeve. "You'll die if you go in there. Then we'll die."

Brie openly wept.

Rand sat up and buried his face in his hands. Kate was gone. And if he went after her, he wouldn't last long in the current. He didn't have the strength. Worse, he'd seal the girls' and Eb's fate, too. Serene was right. They would all wind up tragic victims of the elements.

By pulling him to safety, the girls made the only choice they could. They'd saved his life and theirs and Eb's. He wouldn't wish that decision on anyone, much less two twelve year olds.

Rand shook as a wrenching sob broke free.

The girls stood, perhaps giving him some privacy.

"You gonna be okay?" Serene asked.

What she really wanted to know was, would he leave them to go after Kate?

"Yeah." A bald-faced lie. He'd never be okay again.

The girls left to join Eb, but Rand felt their eyes on him.

After a moment, he gathered his legs beneath him. They responded slowly, as if the signals his brain sent were scrambled. Eventually, he hobbled to the edge of the river.

Cupping his hands around his mouth, he yelled, "Kate!"

What if she'd survived? Would she be able to swim to shore? Reach a shallow spot and pull herself to safety?

Maybe they could ride the horses along the water's edge until they found her. Where did the ravine end? He tried to picture it and couldn't, his fuzzy brain refusing to cooperate.

"Kate! Kate!" The ground shifted beneath his feet, and his vision wavered. Rand grabbed a tree branch to steady himself.

Someone might find her. He had to have faith. The

rain had stopped. County workers would be out conducting inspections and assessing damage.

But that wouldn't be till morning, he realized with despair. Hours and hours from now.

He took a step toward the water and imagined floating down the river to Kate. Him rescuing her and the two of them collapsing onto the bank.

"There's nothing you or any of us can do," Eb said from behind him. "She's a mile away by now."

Rand didn't turn around.

"I know what you're thinking, but she's gone." Eb put an arm on Rand's shoulder. "I hope I'm wrong."

Rand closed his eyes as sadness filled him.

Why, Lord? Why did You bring her to me, allow me to care for her, just to take her away from me?

"I'm sorry, buddy," Eb said in a choked voice. "Truly. But you need to pull yourself together and get the rest of us out of here. The horses are gone. We're on foot."

"They are?" Rand looked around. He hadn't noticed the horses disappearing. Without them, they had no way to go after Kate.

"We aren't going to last another day," Eb said. "We have to reach the trail. You're the only one who can get us there."

Rand swallowed. He wasn't ready to leave. Not yet.

"She'd want you to save us. She'd tell you that if she were here."

A dam broke inside him, and tears filled his eyes. Loss poured out of him, greater than when the doctors told him he wouldn't walk again, leaving him empty. The space was instantly filled with a grief from which he would never recover.

Kate was gone. What was left of his broken heart cried out at the impossibility of a world without her.

He hated the tiny rational part of his mind that admitted Eb was right. Kate would want him to carry on without her. She'd say God wouldn't want Rand to sacrifice three lives for her. That she wasn't worth saving.

Except she'd be wrong. Kate was worth so much more than she'd believed. *Had been* worth so much more.

Lord, why couldn't You have taken me instead?

Serene's and Brie's voices roused him. He barely felt the chilly air or the fiery arrows of pain shooting up his legs as he and Eb stumbled over the rocks toward the girls. He shut down emotionally and physically and mentally. It was the only way he'd be able to function and leave the last place he'd seen Kate alive.

"I won't forget you," he murmured, grieved by thoughts of her and the life together they might have had. A life he hadn't realized he wanted until it was taken from him.

"Which way, Rand?" Eb asked.

He and the girls were standing beside him. Where had they come from?

"We climb out of here and find the trail," he heard himself say in a stranger's voice and as if from a distance. "Then, we head south and follow the markers to the trailhead."

"How far?"

"I don't know. A few miles."

Rand took the lead. Serene and Brie helped Eb, each of them holding on to one of his arms. Though the ravine was less steep in this spot, the going was excruciatingly slow. At the top, they rested for several minutes. The trail lay thirty feet away. Which trail, Rand couldn't be sure until they found a marker. He'd never been this far south.

They shuffled along in silence, downtrodden and disheartened. An hour later, from out of the darkness, large blurry forms appeared before them.

"What's that?" Serene asked.

Eb whistled. "Well, I'll be."

Rand's head shot up. Kate!

But it wasn't her. The miners? Had they gone through all this, lost Kate, just to perish by gunfire?

"It's the horses!" Brie cried.

The herd stood in a group as if waiting for them.

"Thank God," Eb said.

Yes, thank God. If only Kate was with them.

"Can you catch them again?" Serene asked.

Rand pulled himself together. "I can try."

"I'll help."

He studied the girl. She looked different. Older. Wiser.

"All right. Do what I say. No fooling around like with Goliath."

"Right."

He believed her. "Eb, you and Brie wait here. Block the trail in case the horses run this way."

"Count on us." The older man moved next to Brie.

Rand went first and approached the horses slowly. He felt Kate's presence. Heard her whisper to him.

"Easy, Sugar."

As herd leader, the mare was the logical choice. She still wore the fanny pack around her neck. If he could get close enough to her and grab hold of it, they'd have a good chance of riding her again.

"What do you want me to do?" Serene asked in a loud whisper.

"Go left. I'll go right."

As it turned out, the horses didn't need much coaxing. In a short time they'd become used to people. That, or they didn't view Rand and Serene as much of a threat.

If the miners reappeared, they wouldn't view Rand and the others as much of a threat, either. Rand had to get everyone to safety fast.

"That's it, Sugar. Good girl." He slipped his hand beneath the strap around her neck.

The mare snorted and shuffled her feet. Her colt stared at Rand but didn't bolt.

He was glad they'd found the horses and not just because they were no longer on foot. He'd disliked the idea of Sugar and the swayback having to wear a fanny pack and belt around their necks for the rest of their lives. There were dangers associated with that, strangulation chief among them.

Rand wanted more than anything to go in search of Kate. They had the horses. But they would have to travel for hours and hours, hungry and thirsty and having no idea where to look for her. The trailhead was closer. And a search and rescue team no doubt waited for them. They had the manpower and the resources and the stamina to search for Kate or, if Eb was right, her body.

With the heaviest of hearts, Rand called to Serene. Soon afterward, the four of them were mounted and heading south on the trail—Rand and Brie in front on the swayback, Serene and Eb on Sugar. The four remaining horses brought up the rear, walking nose to tail.

Rand found a marker almost immediately. They were on the right trail. Another gift from above. Just as the eastern horizon was changing from black to purple, signaling the approach of dawn, they rounded a bend and the trailhead came into view.

"Look," Serene shouted with glee and pointed. "Trucks and people and horses."

Rand reined the swayback to a stop and stared. He recognized the logo on the side of one of the trucks— the county's mounted search and rescue team. He'd helped them on more than one occasion. With the start of a new, rainless day, a search for them was being launched. Murry and Scotty were there. Knowing them, they would have insisted on accompanying the search party. They'd probably spent the night at the trailhead rather than return to the ranch with the kids.

Ansel was likely at the hospital with Cayden. He'd feel responsible. He might also have the unpleasant task of calling Serene and Brie's foster parents to advise them the girls were missing. As well as Kate's brother, whom she'd listed as her emergency contact.

Who would call to tell him about Kate being carried away by the raging water? Her death? Would her brother even care? Would any of her family care?

Rand's chest tightened. This was all his fault. He'd agreed to let her cross the rushing water on foot. It was a decision he'd regret until his dying day.

"We're saved," Brie shouted and hugged Rand from behind, only to burst into tears. "I wish Kate was here."

"Me, too," Serene murmured.

"That's a sight for sore eyes," Eb said, his voice thick with emotion.

Rand wanted to be happy. Relieved. Thankful.

And he was, for the others. God had seen them safely home. Save for one.

Rand glanced a last time over his shoulder before

nudging the swayback forward. He wouldn't be returning to the Superstitions for a long, long time. If ever.

Kate lost count how many times her head was plunged under the surface. With each submergence, she swallowed more grimy-tasting water. Just as her lungs were about to burst from lack of oxygen, the merciless current flung her to the surface. She gasped as air rushed in—only to be plunged beneath the water for yet another punishing round of torture.

Her arms and legs thrashed uselessly as she tried to swim. She was no match for nature's forces. Boulders slammed into her, pummeling her flesh. Sharp branches scraped her face. Lights flashed in front of her eyes.

Little by little, all the strength drained from her. The edges of her mind went fuzzy. Death was close and about to claim her. Kate would be with her Lord and savior. But there was so much she'd be leaving behind. So many unfulfilled hopes and dreams. Severed relationships with family and friends never to be repaired. Love unexplored. Children never to be born.

She'd miss Rand. Would he miss her?

Too late now. Kate was dying. Something hard and heavy slammed into her back like a battering ram. She screamed, except no sound came out.

And, suddenly, her head broke the water's surface.

Kate woke herself with a terrible coughing fit. It had been a dream, she told herself. She hadn't nearly drowned. God had spared her.

Except her drenched clothes and watery breathing told a different story.

She became aware of her surroundings by degrees. A

roaring filled her ears. Rushing water. When she tried to move, the frightening reality of her predicament became clear. She was still in the wash, wedged in the grip of a fallen tree. While her head and shoulders were above water, the rest of her remained a victim of the ruthless current intent on dragging her into its murky depths.

How long had she been unconscious? More importantly, could she free herself and find her way to solid ground?

She reached out with her right hand and explored the tree that had saved her life. When her feeble fingers closed around a small branch, it instantly broke. The tree was rotten with age. Only the trunk was strong enough to hold her. It acted like a barricade, the current pressing her against the tree and holding her in place.

When she attempted to twist left, she discovered a spike had pierced the material of her jacket. Every effort to free herself failed. The spike refused to release her.

It seemed Kate hadn't been spared after all. Her death was merely delayed.

"Help. Help." Her voice came out a feeble whisper.

Who would hear her out here? No one, other than God. She prayed to Him, asking that she go swiftly and without pain.

Did it hurt to die? Was the everlasting peace people talked about no more than a saying to comfort the living?

"I'm afraid, Lord. I know You're here with me, and I'm grateful for Your presence. But I'm still afraid."

Kate closed her eyes and waited for the serenity God would surely send in her last moments alive on Earth. Her mind drifted. Time faded in and out.

Suddenly—or was it hours later?—she felt hands on

her. Gentle at first, they skimmed across her head and neck. Strange, the hands felt so real. But that was impossible.

"You're all right."

The voice was light and airy and unfamiliar. Kate tilted her head to better hear. At least she wouldn't be alone at the end.

"Hang on. I've got you."

Kate's eyes sprang open. The voice was definitely human, as were the hands now digging into her flesh. This was real!

"Who are you?" she croaked just as the hands hooked her beneath her arms and pulled. Kate stiffened.

"Relax. Don't fight me," her rescuer said.

She was slowly elevated from the water. Branches dug into her back as the person dragged her across the rough tree trunk. Another coughing fit consumed Kate as she was dumped onto the rocky shore of the wash, her bare feet still dangling in the water.

"How bad are you hurt?" the voice asked.

"I... I don't know."

Kate tried to move. Her sluggish limbs were slow to respond. A face loomed over her, its features hidden by a ball cap worn low on their brow. Fingers traveled the length of Kate's body, tenderly assessing any damage.

"Who are you?" she repeated, a memory tapping at the corner of her mind. She'd seen a ball cap recently. When was that? And where?

"Josie," the woman said and lifted Kate to a sitting position. "My name is Josie, and I'm getting you out of here."

"I'm Kate."

"Nice to meet you, Kate."

A rush of dizziness knocked her sideways. She moaned and held her head in both hands. "I'm going to be sick."

"It's okay. Take your time."

When the dizziness subsided, she lifted her face and studied Josie. The memory came into sharp focus. The two hikers. "I know you. We met on the trail."

Josie nodded. "I've been following your group for days."

"We spotted you. Why didn't you join us?"

Her face crumpled before she composed herself. "I was afraid. My husband had been killed. I wasn't sure who to trust."

Kate nodded. She'd feel the same.

"I saw you go under when you were crossing the wash. I wasn't sure I could catch up to you. That water is fast."

"Getting trapped in the log probably helped."

"Don't take this the wrong way," Josie said tentatively, "but I kind of figured you'd be dead."

"I can't believe I'm not."

"Someone's watching over you, for sure."

Sadness flooded Kate's heart. "I'm sorry about your husband. We found his…him."

"The miners killed him." Josie swallowed, distressed anew at the memory. "He died so I could get away."

"Oh." Kate lowered her head and said a silent prayer asking God to keep Josie's husband by His side. "That was incredibly brave of him. And selfless."

"He was a good man. A kind man. He loved me. And he didn't deserve to die. I want the miners to pay." Josie stood. "And the only way for that to happen is for us to report them to the authorities. We have to get out of here to do that."

"I…" Kate felt so stupid. Josie had lost her husband, a good man who'd loved her. "I'm not sure I can. I'm pretty weak."

"It's not that far. Two miles tops. Maybe three."

"I… I lost my boots and socks. One sock, I guess." She'd used the other on Eb's injured leg.

Josie hauled Kate fully out of the water and stood her upright. Kate had to hold on to Josie to keep from falling over as another, albeit milder, wave of dizziness struck. When it passed, the other woman studied Kate's bare feet, pale and wrinkled from being submerged for so long in the water.

"Not a problem."

"Seriously, Josie. I won't last a quarter mile." The rocky desert floor would cut her feet to shreds.

"Put your right hand on my left shoulder," she instructed.

"What?"

"Do as I say. And relax. Let me do the work."

"The work?"

Josie bent at the knees and angled her body. As if Kate were a small child, she lifted and draped Kate across her shoulders in the same way soldiers carried their wounded comrades.

Kate let out a surprised squeak and floundered. "Josie!"

"Don't fight me. I won't drop you." Josie shifted, centering Kate, and then started walking.

"You can't carry me the entire way."

"I can. My husband and I have had a lot of endurance training. I'm stronger than I look."

Kate remembered the heavy backpacks she and her

husband had been carrying and hoped that was true, for they had a long way to go.

"I'm praying for you, Josie."

"That's fine. But it'll be light in a few hours. I'd rather you pray that the miners or the lowlife deputy sheriff they're in partnership with don't find us before we reach help."

Rand and Ansel stood in front of the office at Still Water Ranch, watching the small parade of local law enforcement vehicles leave. Not only had the sheriff's department arrived in force, the police had as well, and one forest service officer. Rand had repeated his story a half-dozen times since this morning.

It wouldn't stop there. Tomorrow, a police sketch artist would work with Rand on a likeness of the miner. Rand hadn't been able to give much of a description of the deputy sheriff. The man had been too far away, and Rand was lying flat on the ground, hiding behind a bush.

Sooner or later, the corrupt deputy sheriff would be caught. Through a process of elimination, if nothing else. How many deputy sheriffs had been driving the Superstitions that day? A check of GPS trackers in official vehicles would narrow the field of suspects.

Ansel clapped Rand on the back. "Dinner will be ready soon. Cook's fixed your favorite. Albondigas soup and flan for dessert."

"I'm not hungry."

"You need to eat, Rand. You went days without a single bite."

"Any word on the search for Kate?"

Ansel shook his head. "They'll let us know the second they find her."

Or find her body. Rand knew enough about search and rescue operations like this one. After twenty-four hours, the odds of locating someone alive dwindled to near zero.

What if they never found her or even any sign of her?

The invisible fist that had been punching him since early this morning buried itself deep in his gut. He nearly doubled over.

"I should have gone after her," he said, hating himself.

"Nothing you could have done, son. You made the only choice you could."

"I should have insisted she ride the mare and cross the wash myself on foot."

"You can't know what would have happened. Kate was a stubborn gal and very determined. She believed she was in better physical shape and the better choice."

Was. Ansel had already started to refer to Kate in the past tense. So had everyone else.

The empty hole inside Rand's gut grew bigger. He wished he'd kept Sugar, her colt and the swayback. Then he'd have had something tangible to remember Kate by. But the head of the search party at the trailhead had decided it was best to turn the horses loose after removing the fanny pack and belt. The small herd depended on Sugar. She was their leader, and they'd struggle to survive without her.

Amazing—or perhaps not, for horses have strong instincts—the four riderless ranch horses had eventually caught up with the rest of the Still Water group after bolting away from Rand, Kate and the girls. When they'd appeared, Scotty had immediately contacted the ranch and reported possible trouble. Which was why the search had been ready to launch the first morning without rain.

They were preparing to mount when Rand, Eb and the girls had rounded the bend on the wild horses. They must have made quite a sight.

After an initial debriefing with the search party and law enforcement called to the scene, Rand had driven home to Still Water Ranch with Scotty. Murry stayed to continue helping with the search.

Rand had wanted to ride out again after a quick bite and some coffee. But, after examining the four of them, the search and rescue medic had refused to clear Rand until he'd had a few proper meals and twelve hours of sleep. Rand would ride out tomorrow if Kate hadn't been found by then.

Did Murry feel guilty about the lousy way he'd treated Kate? Rand did. He'd been wrong about her, and now he'd never have the chance to apologize.

Hadn't that been the whole reason she'd first come to the ranch? To apologize to him? Life could be unfair sometimes and ironic.

"If you don't mind," he said to Ansel, "I'd like some time alone."

"Can you join us after dinner? We're having a prayer meeting for Kate."

"I'll be there." In the meantime, Rand would find a private place to say his own prayers.

Though the Youth Wrangler Camp wasn't ending until tomorrow, the ranch looked deserted. The kids had been asked to stay in the bunkhouses while the authorities were here and to pack their bags in preparation of leaving. Grandpa Billy and a couple of the hands had taken care of the evening chores. For the first time since the inception of Youth Wrangler Camp, the tournament had been canceled.

After returning to the ranch that morning, Serene and Brie had been met by their foster parents, who'd been worried sick. After a touching reunion, and phone calls with their moms and dads, the girls had been questioned by the authorities. They'd surprised Rand with their clear accounts and the seriousness with which they conducted themselves during the interview. They'd matured during the last couple of days. Serene, especially. He held out hope she'd show them all by growing up into a responsible and admirable young adult.

She'd actually asked Ansel about bringing her mom to the ranch for a visit. He'd told her and Brie that they and their families were welcome anytime.

Rand strolled the ranch grounds seeking a private place. He found it at the paddock with Goliath. The normally energetic stallion seemed to sense Rand's somber mood. Rather than whinny and shake his head as he trotted in circles, he walked calmly to the paddock fence, where he rested his big head on the top railing.

Rand scratched the stallion between the ears. "Hey, boy."

Goliath blew out a breath and closed his eyes.

They remained like that for a long time, helping each other to calm the storms raging inside them. Rand prayed. At least, he tried to pray. Those last moments, when the water carried Kate away and her head disappeared beneath the surface, kept replaying in his mind. Could she swim? He didn't know. They'd planned on getting to know each other better when their ordeal ended and they were home safe.

Except, Kate wasn't home. She was lost somewhere in the Superstitions. Maybe in the middle of the desert. When an image of her lifeless form caught in those large iron grates that prevented natural debris from entering the city's canal system sprang to his mind, a ragged sob burst free from his chest.

No. He had to have hope. No news was good news, right?

The stallion's soothing presence helped to keep Rand from falling apart. He dug a bandana from his jeans pocket and used it to wipe his nose. Sounds of people gathering for dinner around the campfire reached his ears. He wasn't hungry but should probably join them and force himself to eat. If not, he wouldn't be allowed to join the search tomorrow. Plus, he wouldn't miss the prayer meeting.

Every bone in his body ached, not just his legs. The medic had advised him to see a doctor, but he'd refused. Nothing wrong with him that a few days of rest wouldn't fix. And seeing Kate again.

"Take it easy, boy." He gave Goliath a final pat. "I need to get going."

"There you are."

Rand turned to see Ansel approaching. The shadow from his cowboy hat covered most of his face, preventing Rand from reading his boss's expression.

He had a bad feeling and steeled himself.

"Been looking for you," Ansel said as he drew nearer. "The sheriff's office called. There's news."

No! Don't tell me. I don't want to hear it. They are wrong.

Rand retreated a step, his heart grinding to a stop. He tried to speak, but his throat had completely closed. No air could escape.

Ansel held out a small paper sack. "Here. You're going to need this."

Rand glanced away, refusing to look.

"We're not leaving until you take it."

A minute. He needed a minute.

Ansel must have brought Rand's Bible, anticipating a need for comforting passages. Or was it something of Kate's? A personal item to remember her by?

His eyes drifted to his boss, then, gathering all his courage, he sought the item. Finally, he found his voice. "Leave for where?"

"The hospital. You can eat this on the way." Ansel pressed the sack into Rand's chest. "It's a ham-and-cheese sandwich and some sugar cookies. Can't have you passing out from hunger."

"The hospital," Rand repeated lamely. "Why, Ansel?" He grabbed his boss's arm. "Is it Kate? Did they find her? Is she in the morgue?"

Did they expect Rand to identify her body?

Ansel cracked a smile. "No. She's not in the morgue."

Hope, and then joy, exploded inside Rand.

"She's alive, son. And I'm told she's going to be all right. I'm also told she's asking for you."

Rand dropped to his knees.

Thank You, Lord. Thank You, thank You.

Five minutes later, he and Ansel were headed to the hospital.

Chapter Fourteen

"What's that?" Kate asked when a stocky male nurse set a tiny paper cup on her overbed table next to her empty dinner plate. To call her meal mediocre would be a stretch, yet she'd inhaled every bite and almost requested seconds.

"Just something to help you sleep tonight." The nurse gave her a jovial grin and checked her IV port. She'd been prescribed intravenous antibiotics—a precaution in case she'd picked up a bacterial infection in the massive amount of dirty water she'd swallowed while nearly drowning. "Doctor's orders. Take it when you're ready."

"I don't think I need anything to help me sleep. I'm exhausted."

The closest she'd come to a nap was when she drifted in and out while Josie carried her to a utility company truck parked alongside a lonely stretch of dirt road. Kate would never forget the startled look on the worker's face when he saw them emerge from behind a tall saguaro cactus. The bag of peanuts and warm can of soda he'd offered them was the most delicious food Kate had ever tasted.

"You say that now." The nurse checked her bedside monitors. "Hospitals are noisy at night. Plus, someone will be in every few hours waking you up to check your vitals and draw blood. The pill will help you fall back to sleep."

"Do they have to wake me up?"

"Sorry. More doctor's orders. You gave everybody quite a scare."

Kate laid her head back on the pillow and sighed. "Okay."

"Considering everything you went through, you're in amazing shape. Though, your oxygen levels are a bit low. We need to watch for any fluids in your lungs."

"I feel weak as a newborn pup."

"You'll be your old self in no time, once your sprains and bruising have healed."

She'd been fortunate. If things had gone differently, she'd have wound up like Josie's husband, her body tossed behind some boulders. Kate had learned from Josie the gunshot they'd heard that first night in camp had taken his life. They'd been right to be concerned and post guards.

Dear Lord, watch over Josie. She needs You now in this, her darkest hour.

"What about my friend?" Kate asked. "Have the doctors released her yet? I'd like to see her."

"I'm not sure." The nurse gave Kate a pat on the arm. "I'll find out for you. The authorities were still interviewing her last I heard. We haven't had this much excitement since quadruplets were born here last winter. Which reminds me, there are reporters in the lobby wanting to interview you."

"Not now." Kate shook her head. She didn't know when, if ever, she'd feel ready to speak to the news.

"Don't worry. Hospital protocol. No one gets past the front desk unless they're experiencing a medical emergency."

"Thank you."

"Illegal miners. Who'd have thought, huh? Like there aren't enough weird stories already about those mountains."

A soft rap on the door interrupted them.

Kate glanced up, and it was as if a burst of sunlight filled the room. Rand stood there, a worried expression on his handsome face. A flood of emotions cascaded through her, the most prominent of them joy. They'd made it out of the Superstitions alive, like he'd promised. Not together, but that didn't matter. He was here now.

"Can I come in?" he asked.

"Yes." She sat up, ignoring the slight dizziness brought on by her sudden movement. "Please."

"Ah." The nurse grinned broadly. "You must be the fellow who single-handedly brought that man and two girls out on wild horses."

Rand stepped into the room. He removed his cowboy hat but didn't take his eyes off Kate. "Not single-handedly. We all worked together. It's incredible what a person's capable of when fighting for their life. Kate is a warrior."

She laughed. "I did call myself that, didn't I?"

He smiled. "I'm awfully glad to see you."

Her insides melted in response. "Same here."

"I think I'll leave you two alone." The nurse rehung the clipboard on Kate's bed. "Don't keep her up too late," he warned Rand. "She's had a rough day and needs her sleep."

"A few rough days," Rand clarified. "And I won't."

Once the nurse had left, he hung his hat on the back of the visitor chair and approached. Kate didn't think, she simply opened her arms to him. He went to her and gathered her up, holding her as tightly as she held him. She buried her face in his shoulder, reveling in the sensation of his strong embrace.

This feels like home.

They didn't speak for several moments. Rather, they let their hearts do the talking.

When at last they broke apart, Rand cupped her cheek in his large palm. "I thought I lost you."

She saw the tears in his eyes and blinked back her own. "I have to admit, I was scared for a while there."

"Me, too." He bent and kissed her then, briefly, his lips soft on hers. "I've been wanting to do that for a while now."

"Not when I first came to Still Water Ranch."

"I was wrong. I owe you an apology. Holding on to my anger was a habit. A bad one."

"I ruined your life."

"You didn't." He traced his thumb along her jawline. "You gave me a brand-new life, Kate. And I thank you."

She hesitated and then poured out her heart. "The accident changed the course of our lives. In terrible ways. You were hurt. I spent years in prison. But, for me, I found a strength and faith I didn't have before. We can't know for sure, but I believe I'm better off, and a better person, than if I'd walked away that day. I only wish you hadn't been hurt. It's my greatest regret."

"Don't beat yourself up. Our lives did change. I know

mine did for the better. Especially because we found our way back to each other." He pressed his lips to hers for another kiss that lingered. When he at last released her, he pulled the visitor chair close to her bed and sat. "I can't remember ever being so scared, Kate. Not even after the accident when I didn't know if I'd walk again. I was afraid you'd been taken from me, and I couldn't bear the thought…" His voice broke.

"I wasn't, Rand. I'm right here."

"Thank God."

"Yes. If not for Him and Josie and the horses, who knows what would have happened to any of us."

"It's terrible about her husband," Rand said. "How's she doing?"

Kate shivered at the memory of Josie's husband's life-less body. "As well as anyone can, I suppose. I'm hoping she'll stop by my room before she leaves the hospital."

"Did she say how she escaped the miners?"

"She and her husband chose a place to camp for the night close to the miners' cave. Of course, they had no clue it was filled with explosives and supplies. While her husband made camp, she went looking for dry fire-wood. The miners apparently returned, considered him a threat and ambushed him. He didn't give her away, though." Kate wiped at a tear. "Rand, he saved her."

"He was a hero."

"She realized the danger before reaching their camp and hid. Her husband must have convinced the miners he was alone because they never went looking for her. When she heard the gunshot and the miners talking, she knew her husband was dead. She got scared after that and ran."

"It's a good thing she did."

"She feels guilty about not saving him."

"There's nothing she could have done," Rand said. "The miners would have killed her, too."

"That's what I told her. But forgiving yourself isn't easy. I can vouch for that."

Rand lifted one of Kate's hands and pressed a kiss to it. "You have nothing to be forgiven for."

"I've made my peace. I pray Josie will, too, one day. I don't believe for a second her husband would have wanted her to die alongside him. Given the chance, I'm sure he would have insisted she save herself."

Rand nodded. "Did she really carry you all the way out?"

"Two miles over some pretty rugged terrain."

"I'm impressed."

"She and her husband are, were, endurance hikers. Plus, she's determined the miners will pay for what they did to him. She said she needed me to be a witness and would have carried me for days if necessary."

"She's incredibly brave. And strong."

"She also ate better than us. She had some trail mix and beef jerky and dried fruit in her backpack."

"Remind me before the next trail ride to buy a backpack and fill it with food."

"Why don't we just not get separated during a storm again?"

He chuckled. "I like that idea better."

"Me, too."

"In fact," Rand said, his feelings for her evident in his loving gaze, "I'm not letting you out of my sight for a long time."

Kate returned his gaze, emotion for emotion. "Sounds

good to me." When he released her hand, she asked, "How are Serene and Brie?"

"Good. Both of them feel bad and blame themselves. Serene, especially. She says if she hadn't stolen my phone, none of this would have happened."

"Poor kid. She was desperate to talk to her mom."

"She thinks God won't forgive her. That because of her, Eb was injured and you almost drowned."

"I'm glad to see her taking responsibility. It shows maturity. But she's not to blame."

"If anyone's responsible, I am," Rand insisted. "I should have turned us around and headed home at the first sign of rain."

"Your intentions were in the right place. The trail ride is a camp tradition. You wanted to show the kids a good time and teach them not only outdoor skills but how to deal with unexpected circumstances, like weather. Serene wanted to make sure her mom was okay. If you ask Ansel, he's blaming himself, too, for not canceling the ride."

Rand blew out a breath. "I'm going to need to say a few prayers and do a few good deeds before I forgive myself."

"Oh, Rand." Kate felt sorry for him and knew what he was going through. "You do good deeds daily. God knows your heart, and He doesn't hold you responsible. No one does. There's nothing to forgive."

He shrugged. "I'm glad no one was hurt worse than they were."

"Which reminds me. How's Eb?"

"Doing great. Doctors sewed up his leg. Nothing vital was damaged. They thought for a minute he might need a transfusion but decided whoever bound his leg on the trail did a good job."

Kate smiled. "What about Cayden?"

"The kid sailed through surgery. He's excited about having a cast and his ribcage taped and telling anyone who will listen about his fall and being airlifted out in a medical helicopter. His family is with him now."

"What a relief." Kate said a silent prayer of thanks.

"Serene and Brie's foster parents are with them at the ranch now. They were going to take the girls home today, but Serene and Brie want to wait until tomorrow and leave with the rest of the kids. Ansel got their foster parents a room at the Superstition Vista Motel for the night."

"That's nice of him."

Rand hesitated.

"What?" Kate asked.

"It's none of my business, but have you talked to your family yet?"

"No."

"Ansel called your brother while we were missing. You listed him as your emergency contact."

"Oh."

"He called him again to tell him you were all right and gave him the name of the hospital."

She nodded, a lump in her throat.

Rand captured her hand again. "This might be a good time to reach out to them."

"It might." She remembered being carried along by the raging current, thinking that she was going to die, and regretting her estrangement from her family. Was God sending her a message through Rand? It was possible.

"Excuse me for interrupting."

At the authoritative male voice, Kate and Rand looked up to see a uniformed deputy sheriff standing at the door.

"I'm Deputy Armando Herrera. If you have a minute," he said, "I'd like to talk to you."

Rand stood the instant the deputy sheriff entered Kate's hospital room. Despite seeing various law enforcement individuals throughout the day, his nerves hummed, and his pulse hammered.

"Come in." Kate motioned to the deputy.

He tugged on the brim of his hat. "Thank you."

"Would you care to sit?" Rand offered him the visitor chair.

"No. That's quite all right. I won't be long. I was here interviewing Mr. Ebersol when I received an update. Thought I'd fill Ms. Spencer in before I returned to the station." The man's lined cheeks and pronounced crow's feet were testament to a lifetime spent in the Arizona outdoors. "How are you doing, ma'am?" he asked Kate.

"Much better. Now."

"I'm Rand Walkins." Rand stepped forward. "I spoke to a Deputy Johnston this morning."

"Yes. He and I conferred earlier. Good to meet you." Deputy Herrera shook Rand's hand, his grip firm and no-nonsense.

"What's happened?" Kate asked. "Have you arrested the miners?"

"Not yet, sorry to say. The CSI team is searching the cave with a fine-tooth comb. We're working with local police and the FBI, following leads. It won't be long, though. Thanks to the information you both provided—" he nodded at Rand "—we have the deputy you spotted in custody and are questioning him."

"Wow." Rand was impressed. "That didn't take long."

"Our tech team got right on it."

"Did the deputy give you the miners' names and location?" Kate asked.

The deputy's gaze traveled from her to Rand and back. "Sorry, I can't reveal any details about an ongoing investigation. But I assure you, we'll be in touch soon."

"I understand." Rand did. And he'd put it in God's hands to see that justice was served.

"Well, it's late." Deputy Herrera nodded. "I won't keep you. Thank you again for your help. And job well done getting out of those mountains in one piece. Not everyone could have managed it."

"Thank you for your hard work," Kate said. "Those miners killed an innocent man."

"We're going to do our best to find them."

Minutes after the deputy left, Ansel appeared carrying an arrangement of fresh flowers that had probably come from the hospital gift shop.

"Hey, there." He greeted Kate with a huge grin.

"Thank you, Ansel. Those are beautiful."

"I'm happy to see you're not looking too worse for the wear." He set the vase on her overbed table.

Kate laughed and brushed self-consciously at her hair. "Please don't hand me a mirror because I'll know you're lying."

Acknowledging Rand, he moved close and bent to give Kate a brief hug. When he spoke, his voice held a gruff edge. "Mighty glad to see you."

"And I'm glad to see you."

"I'm only staying a minute. I just wanted to check on you and ask if there's anything you need. Anything at all."

"I'm fine. Nothing I can think of."

"Well, if you change your mind, just call."

"I will."

"And when they let you out of here, I want to talk to you about a permanent job at Still Water. At least extend your trial period. You didn't really give us a proper test drive." He winked at her and Rand. "I'm also thinking things maybe changed between the two of you, and you're more receptive to staying on than you were before."

"Well, I…"

"She is," Rand said, answering for her.

Ansel did a poor job of hiding his pleasure. "That's fine. Mighty fine. You're putting a spring in this old man's step." He turned to Rand. "I'll wait for you in the lobby. No hurry. But before I leave, do you two mind if I say a prayer?"

Kate smiled. "I'd like that."

He and Rand stood beside Kate's bed, and the three of them joined hands. Ansel spoke softly but with genuine emotion.

"Lord, Your powers are great, and that was never more evident than these last few days. We thank You for giving Kate, Rand, Serene, Brie and Dermot Ebersol Your protection and bringing them safely home. We ask that You watch over Josie, whose strength and courage saved our dear Kate's life when she might have otherwise perished. Please assist the authorities in their search for the illegal miners, who not only destroyed precious natural resources but took a man's life. And, lastly, we thank You for helping Rand and Kate heal from their troubled pasts and make peace with each other. And who knows, Lord, maybe something more will come out of this. Because if there were ever two people who deserved forgiveness and to find love, it's them. May we live in the shining light of Your grace. Amen."

"Amen." Rand opened his eyes to catch a quick glance at Kate. If she was surprised by the last part of Ansel's prayer, she didn't let on.

"I'll see you tomorrow." Ansel tweaked her chin and patted Rand's shoulder.

Once he'd left, Rand sat again in the visitor chair. "So, did the doctor say when you're getting out of here?"

"I'm hoping in the morning."

"Any possibility we can go to dinner one night soon? When you're feeling better."

"Dinner? Like a...date?"

"Yeah. A date."

"I know things were a little frantic back there in the shelter, and it's possible I misunderstood you, but didn't we agree to start with simply working together and see how that went?"

Rand chuckled. "That's what dating is all about. Getting to know each other better. Charlie's Chuck Box has great mesquite-grilled steaks and chicken. If you like that kind of food."

He waited, growing a little anxious when she didn't immediately reply. Had he moved too fast? Assumed too much? He attempted to bow out gracefully.

"Hey, look. If you're not interested, no big deal."

"I like that kind of food," she said tentatively.

"All right. Then, did I misread—"

"It's not that."

"I get that I treated you badly last week. And you're probably wondering how my feelings could have changed so quickly."

"I'm not. My feelings have changed, too. So, I understand."

He let himself relax.

"I haven't dated a whole lot," Kate continued. "With my history, well, it's not been easy. Guys are a little reluctant to get involved with a former felon."

"Their loss."

She smiled.

"I mean it."

"The thing is, I take dating and relationships seriously. Which probably sounds unexpected coming from me."

"It doesn't. I take dating seriously, too."

"I want a future with someone one day. Marriage. A family. I'm not trying to scare you off. I'm letting you know where I stand should you have different goals."

Rand reached out and tucked a strand of hair behind her ear. "I want those things too, Kate. One day."

She nodded.

"Look, we aren't in any rush. After a few months, when I'm head over heels for you and you think I'm the greatest guy there ever was, we'll get serious."

"You sound confident."

"I am confident. I care about you, Kate. Enough that I believe we have what it takes for the long haul. And I'm confident you care about me, too."

"I might," she teased.

"God has a purpose for bringing us together. I'm willing to see what He has in mind."

"You make me happy, Rand. And I haven't been happy in a very long time."

He leaned in and kissed her, her soft lips melting against his in a celebration of all the possibilities that lay before them. They had survived a terrible ordeal and come out on the other side changed for the better and ready to embrace a future filled with potential.

Epilogue

One Year Later

Rand and Ansel watched as a dozen kids attempted to saddle their horses under Grandpa Billy's supervision. The youngsters fumbled with the straps and buckles, giggled nervously, tried to one-up each other and had to be told everything at least twice.

Ansel chuckled. "Different faces, same kids. Year after year. I should retire."

"You love Youth Wrangler Camp. You'll never retire."

"I will eventually." He gave Rand an elbow jab in the side. "Then, you'll be in charge."

"Maybe."

"Right."

They both knew Rand would. He made it a practice of paying forward his good fortune, and the Youth Wrangler Camp was one of his favorite ways.

"Not like that," Serene scolded and took over bridling Flapjack from one of the rookie members. "See this opening? You put his ears through it like that."

"We're going to make a cowgirl out of her yet," Ansel nodded approvingly.

"She likes it here," Rand said. "She likes you. You're good to her."

"Some of God's children are like flowers in the shade. They just need a little sunshine to bloom. That's Serene."

Soon after Serene returned to her foster parents last summer, her dad stopped drinking and got a job. Seemed nearly losing his daughter was the kick in the pants he'd needed to make changes. Though the situation with her parents had improved, Serene still lived full-time in foster care. She did, however, visit her parents on weekends and holidays. If all went well, she'd exit the foster care system soon—like Brie had several months earlier.

Both girls were regular visitors to Still Water Ranch. Ansel had made an exception and invited them to return this summer as senior members of the Youth Wrangler Camp, but only Serene could attend. Brie was visiting her grandparents in California.

"By the way, I have something for you." Ansel dug out his wallet from his back pocket, removed a folded slip of paper and passed it to Rand. "Your share from the sale of the sorrel mare."

"Thank you, boss." Rand opened the check, glanced at the amount and whistled. "This is way more than we agreed on."

"The amount includes a fifty percent down payment on the buckskin yearling."

"No fooling!"

Ansel grinned. "No fooling."

They'd formed a partnership this past winter. Ansel funded the money to adopt feral horses captured by the

Bureau of Land Management in the Salt River Valley area, horses like Sugar and the swayback. Rand trained them, and once they were sold, he and Ansel split the profits.

"I can use this." Rand pocketed the check. "I've had a few big expenses lately."

"One in particular."

"That's true."

"Life is a series of changes," Ansel mused. "Speaking of which, Grandpa Billy turned in his resignation this morning."

"What? No!"

"Well, he's been ready to retire for a while. Going to live in town with his son and daughter-in-law. Don't you worry. He'll be coming around plenty. Just to cause trouble and get in our hair."

"Glad to hear." Rand would have missed the old guy.

"He had only one request," Ansel continued. "He wanted me to give you the manager's residence. I agreed."

"Seriously, boss?"

"You're entitled. You've had the job for a while—you should have the benefits that go with it."

The manager's residence was a modest two-bedroom house about a quarter mile down the road on the edge of Still Water Ranch. Far enough away for some privacy, and close enough for the manager to arrive quickly in case of emergency. No one had had the heart to ask Grandpa Billy to vacate the house after he stepped down as manager and Rand was promoted.

"I really appreciate that," Rand said, fighting a tightness in his chest.

"You're going to need more room to call your own than a bed in the bunkhouse."

The two of them looked up at the sound of an approaching vehicle, the bright noonday sun reflecting off the windshield. Rand felt a smile form at the sight of Kate's old pickup truck rolling toward them. She really needed something newer and more reliable. He should look into finding her an affordable replacement.

"She's running late," Ansel observed. "Meeting go long?"

"Probably. She has trouble ending on time if one of the members is in crisis."

"I admire her. She's doing God's work."

For the past nine months, Kate led a weekly support group for women recently released from prison. Her friend Rosario, the woman who had first invited Kate to prison services, had formed the group. Kate loved helping and, like Rand, made a practice of paying forward her good fortune.

She and Josie had remained close after their ordeal and got together at least once a month for lunch or a hike in the mountains. Josie had been able to find closure, as much as one could find it, after the three miners had been arrested and taken into custody. As predicted, the deputy sheriff had talked in exchange for a lighter sentence. A two-month manhunt had culminated with the capture of one miner. He led them to the other two.

All three were presently in jail awaiting trial. Josie planned to be there every day. Kate, too, in support of her friend.

She parked the truck near the paddock railing and climbed out. Rand's heart swelled with love at the sight of her. He was a fortunate man. He could have lost her last year. Not only when she'd almost drowned, but before that by refusing to put his anger behind him and stop blaming her for the accident.

"Hey, there," he said.

"Sorry I'm late." She hurried toward them.

Rand pulled her close for a hug and kissed her cheek. "You're fine. The lesson hasn't started yet."

She turned to Ansel. "Is there anything I need to get for dinner tonight?"

The ranch owner and his wife were hosting Kate's parents, brother and sister, along with Rand and Kate. It was an opportunity for her family to meet Rand in a casual, comfortable setting.

"Mrs. Sciacca said she has everything under control," Ansel insisted.

"You sure?"

"You're nervous." He chuckled. "Relax. Everything will be fine."

"I hope so. It's just that...we're still finding our way with each other, and the going has been slow."

"Slow going is better than no going."

Serene's dad wasn't the only one who'd changed after receiving their startling news. Kate's family came to the hospital the day after they heard about her ordeal. Possibly to assuage their guilt. That was what Rand thought, anyway, because the reunion hadn't gone well. She and her family saw each other again, however. And again. They were trying, and that was all anyone could ask.

"Your family will like me," Rand said. "Just like my family likes you." Naturally, they'd been shocked at first to learn he and Kate were dating. Soon, they'd come to feel the same as him: he and Kate were meant to be together.

Rand captured her left hand in his, running his thumb

over the diamond engagement ring on her third finger—something he did frequently since proposing two weeks ago. He liked reminding himself that someday in the near future Kate was going to be his wife.

"I know they'll like you." She gazed at him with those hazel eyes he could spend hours getting lost in. "You can be very charming when you try."

"Only when I try?" he teased.

"All right, you two," Ansel interrupted. "Let's get to work or we won't finish in time for dinner."

He was joking. He wouldn't let anything get in the way of tonight's celebration.

"Thank you again, Ansel." Kate broke away from Rand to give him a quick hug. "You and your wife are the best."

After he left, Rand put an arm around Kate and kissed the top of her head.

"I love you, sweetheart."

"I love you, too."

"I thank God every day that you had the courage to show up here. Because I didn't have the courage to reach out to you when I should have years ago. Maybe then you would have spent less time in prison."

She shook her head. "Let's not dwell on what might have been. Let's rejoice in what is."

"Which we are going to do tonight with your family."

"Yes, we are."

He thought about telling her that Grandpa Billy was retiring, and that Ansel had given him the manager's residence. He decided to wait. That would be yet another reason for them to celebrate tomorrow.

"Kate," Serene called from where the horses and kids stood at the paddock railing. "We're ready."

She sighed. "Duty calls."

"Have a good lesson."

Rand watched her go. After climbing onto Mega Max, she rode the big gelding to the arena, the kids following behind on their mounts.

A moment later, she turned in the saddle and waved, her smile dazzling him.

"Thank You, Lord," he murmured and waved back, marveling again, as he often did, how their lives had come full circle—from heartache to hearts joined together, always and forever.

* * * * *

Get 3 FREE REWARDS!

We'll send you 2 FREE Books plus a FREE Mystery Gift.

FREE Value Over **$20**

Both the **Love Inspired®** and **Love Inspired®** Suspense series feature compelling novels filled with inspirational romance, faith, forgiveness and hope.

YES! Please send me 2 FREE novels from the Love Inspired or Love Inspired Suspense series and my FREE gift (gift is worth about $10 retail). After receiving them, if I don't wish to receive any more books, I can return the shipping statement marked "cancel." If I don't cancel, I will receive 6 brand-new Love Inspired Larger-Print books or Love Inspired Suspense Larger-Print books every month and be billed just $6.49 each in the U.S. or $6.74 each in Canada. That is a savings of at least 16% off the cover price. It's quite a bargain! Shipping and handling is just 50¢ per book in the U.S. and $1.25 per book in Canada.* I understand that accepting the 2 free books and gift places me under no obligation to buy anything. I can always return a shipment and cancel at any time by calling the number below. The free books and gift are mine to keep no matter what I decide.

Choose one: ☐ **Love Inspired Larger-Print** (122/322 BPA GRPA) ☐ **Love Inspired Suspense Larger-Print** (107/307 BPA GRPA) ☐ **Or Try Both!** (122/322 & 107/307 BPA GRRP)

Name (please print)

Address   Apt. #

City   State/Province   Zip/Postal Code

Email: Please check this box ☐ if you would like to receive newsletters and promotional emails from Harlequin Enterprises ULC and its affiliates. You can unsubscribe anytime.

Mail to the Harlequin Reader Service:
IN U.S.A.: P.O. Box 1341, Buffalo, NY 14240-8531
IN CANADA: P.O. Box 603, Fort Erie, Ontario L2A 5X3

Want to try 2 free books from another series? Call 1-800-873-8635 or visit www.ReaderService.com.

*Terms and prices subject to change without notice. Prices do not include sales taxes, which will be charged (if applicable) based on your state or country of residence. Canadian residents will be charged applicable taxes. Offer not valid in Quebec. This offer is limited to one order per household. Books received may not be as shown. Not valid for current subscribers to the Love Inspired or Love Inspired Suspense series. All orders subject to approval. Credit or debit balances in a customer's account(s) may be offset by any other outstanding balance owed by or to the customer. Please allow 4 to 6 weeks for delivery. Offer available while quantities last.

Your Privacy—Your information is being collected by Harlequin Enterprises ULC, operating as Harlequin Reader Service. For a complete summary of the information we collect, how we use this information and to whom it is disclosed, please visit our privacy notice located at corporate.harlequin.com/privacy-notice. From time to time we may also exchange your personal information with reputable third parties. If you wish to opt out of this sharing of your personal information, please visit readerservice.com/consumerchoice or call 1-800-873-8635. **Notice to California Residents**—Under California law, you have specific rights to control and access your data. For more information on these rights and how to exercise them, visit corporate.harlequin.com/california-privacy.

LIRLIS23

Get 3 FREE REWARDS!

We'll send you 2 FREE Books plus a FREE Mystery Gift.

FREE Value Over **$20**

Both the **Harlequin® Special Edition** and **Harlequin® Heartwarming™** series feature compelling novels filled with stories of love and strength where the bonds of friendship, family and community unite.

YES! Please send me 2 FREE novels from the Harlequin Special Edition or Harlequin Heartwarming series and my FREE Gift (gift is worth about $10 retail). After receiving them, if I don't wish to receive any more books, I can return the shipping statement marked "cancel." If I don't cancel, I will receive 6 brand-new Harlequin Special Edition books every month and be billed just $5.49 each in the U.S. or $6.24 each in Canada, a savings of at least 12% off the cover price, or 4 brand-new Harlequin Heartwarming Larger-Print books every month and be billed just $6.24 each in the U.S. or $6.74 each in Canada, a savings of at least 19% off the cover price. It's quite a bargain! Shipping and handling is just 50¢ per book in the U.S. and $1.25 per book in Canada.* I understand that accepting the 2 free books and gift places me under no obligation to buy anything. I can always return a shipment and cancel at any time by calling the number below. The free books and gift are mine to keep no matter what I decide.

Choose one: ☐ **Harlequin Special Edition** (235/335 BPA GRMK)   ☐ **Harlequin Heartwarming Larger-Print** (161/361 BPA GRMK)   ☐ **Or Try Both!** (235/335 & 161/361 BPA GRPZ)

Name (please print)

Address   Apt. #

City   State/Province   Zip/Postal Code

Email: Please check this box ☐ if you would like to receive newsletters and promotional emails from Harlequin Enterprises ULC and its affiliates. You can unsubscribe anytime.

Mail to the Harlequin Reader Service:

IN U.S.A.: P.O. Box 1341, Buffalo, NY 14240-8531
IN CANADA: P.O. Box 603, Fort Erie, Ontario L2A 5X3

Want to try 2 free books from another series! Call 1-800-873-8635 or visit www.ReaderService.com.

*Terms and prices subject to change without notice. Prices do not include sales taxes, which will be charged (if applicable) based on your state or country of residence. Canadian residents will be charged applicable taxes. Offer not valid in Quebec. This offer is limited to one order per household. Books received may not be as shown. Not valid for current subscribers to the Harlequin Special Edition or Harlequin Heartwarming series. All orders subject to approval. Credit or debit balances in a customer's account(s) may be offset by any other outstanding balance owed by or to the customer. Please allow 4 to 6 weeks for delivery. Offer available while quantities last.

Your Privacy—Your information is being collected by Harlequin Enterprises ULC, operating as Harlequin Reader Service. For a complete summary of the information we collect, how we use this information and to whom it is disclosed, please visit our privacy notice located at corporate.harlequin.com/privacy-notice. From time to time we may also exchange your personal information with reputable third parties. If you wish to opt out of this sharing of your personal information, please visit readerservice.com/consumerchoice or call 1-800-873-8635. **Notice to California Residents**—Under California law, you have specific rights to control and access your data. For more information on these rights and how to exercise them, visit corporate.harlequin.com/california-privacy.

HSEHW23

Get 3 FREE REWARDS!

We'll send you 2 FREE Books plus a FREE Mystery Gift.

FREE
Value Over
$20

Both the **Mystery Library** and **Essential Suspense** series feature compelling novels filled with gripping mysteries, edge-of-your-seat thrillers and heart-stopping romantic suspense stories.

HARLEQUIN
PLUS

Try the best multimedia subscription service for romance readers like you!

Read, Watch and Play.

Experience the easiest way to get the romance content you crave.

Start your **FREE TRIAL** at
<u>www.harlequinplus.com/freetrial</u>.